THE

OTHER END

OF THE

TUNNEL

J.L. FREDRICK

First Edition

ISBN: 0974905895
ISBN-13: 978-0974905891
(Previous ISBN: 0759623872)

Printed in the United States of America

Cover design by Lovstad Publishing

Novels by J.L. Fredrick

The Gaslight Knights
Thunder in the Night
The Great Train Robbery of Monroe County
Mad City Bust
September Ten
Aftermath
Cursed by the Wind
Another Shade of Gray
Across the Dead Line
Across the Second Dead Line
The Private Journal of Clancy Crane
The Other End of the Tunnel

Non-Fiction
Rivers, Roads, and Rails

THE

OTHER END

OF THE

TUNNEL

ONE

L ightning drenched the pitch black night sky revealing ominous storm clouds for as far as the eye could see, and the crackling thunder thumped out an irregular rhythm of a nearly constant echoing rumble. Shawn Kelly and Steve Allison rambled southward along the sidewalk past the darkened storefronts of the three-block-long business district of Main Street. They weren't window shopping. They weren't on their way to a party. Shawn Kelly and Steve Allison were about to embark on a planned adventure that anyone else in the entire town would have considered an act of pure insanity.

A few blocks south on Main Street, the stark, weather-beaten Hawthorne mansion occupied a half- acre weed-infested lot, projecting a year-round haunting Halloween atmosphere to the encompassing neighborhood. It had been spared the torment of vandals and the cruelty of graffiti artisans over the years as its drab, paintless form stood an unscathed, untouched hideous landmark that no one wanted to go near. Children were taught to stay away from the unknown evil presence, and there seemed to be an invisible barrier protecting it from visitors who were unaware of its uncanny legend.

The legend was based on the two old spinsters, twins, who had occupied the dwelling since long before the turn of the century. Emma and Lizzy Hawthorne were said by some to be Salem witches, who must have migrated here to escape the perils of eminent doom. Some claimed they were devil worshippers, or maybe even the daughters of Satan, himself. The stories went on to include that night in 1947 when the Hawthorne twins both died on the eve of their 100th birthday, and when their bodies were discovered, they were buried in unmarked graves and forgotten.

There were as many variations to the legend as there were storytellers, but all concluded with one non-conflicting fact: the ghosts of Emma and Lizzy Hawthorne were still present in that house. They had been sighted on countless occasions by dozens of prominent citizens—too many to discount the validity of the claims.

To their knowledge, no one had ever set foot inside the old Hawthorne house for nearly two decades, but the tales it spawned were endless and the legends those stories inspired were nothing short of intrigue to Shawn and Steve. Although many people of Westland were convinced the lore was simply the product of wild imagination, Shawn and Steve were convinced otherwise.

Tonight, the conditions were perfect. The approach of a thunderstorm would provide the one element consistent in *all* the ghostly tales they had ever heard. Every sighting of the Hawthorne ghosts through the third story windows had occurred during late-night thunderstorms, and even they had sensed strange auras in close proximity to the house on many nights like this when they watched in anticipation from across the street in the park. But tonight, they weren't just observing. Tonight they were going in.

At ten o'clock on any other July Friday night in Westland, Main Street would be alive with throngs of youngsters enjoying summer vacation, testing the rules of curfew. But tonight, the intensifying storm had most everyone seeking indoor amusement as Mother Nature spewed out her adversities. Except for the usual flow of traffic, Main Street was nearly deserted.

The rain was just beginning to fall as Shawn and Steve dashed across the park to take shelter in the gazebo next to the rose garden. It would offer them modest protection from the elements while they waited for the right moment, as from there they had a clear view of Main Street in both directions, and a clear view of their object of obsession.

Just across the street stood the decrepit, abandoned Hawthorne house. It reeked of neglect, and even during daylight hours, it levied an eerie presence on the surrounding area, but everyone in the town had learned to ignore it—everyone, that is, except Shawn Kelly and Steve Allison. Their burning desire to explore its interior and to discover its mysterious past was more than just teen-aged mischief. It was curiosity beyond all imagination.

What a grand place it must have once been, but more than twenty years of vacancy and neglect had washed away its elegance. Now the Hawthorne house was the property of the State, as the Hawthorne sisters had left behind no known heirs to their legacy. It was only a matter of time before the old domicile would be toppled from its foundation to make way for the ever-increasing progress of the sixties. No one seemed too concerned about its preservation, but rather, all of Westland looked forward to the day when a more attractive, modern adornment would take its place.

Shawn and Steve were no different from any other youngsters in the community: they clearly remembered the instructions they had received long ago to keep their distance from the house, which they had respectfully heeded most all of their seventeen years... until now. They had never been any closer than the iron gate at the entrance to the front yard, that, for as long as they could remember had always been the snarly, unsightly entanglement of vines and weeds. And until just a couple of days ago when they hid the crow bar in the weeds along the fence next to the railroad tracks, they had never ventured to the back side where they were about to make their approach to gain entrance. All the ground floor windows and the only door on that side of the house were boarded up tightly, but just to the right of the barricaded door was an angled trap door at ground level, the entrance into the cellar, unmistakably their way in. And because there were no street lights to illuminate the back yard, the darkness would veil their presence there. No one would ever notice the disturbed trap door somewhat concealed by the tall weeds.

The rain was coming down harder now and flashes of lightning strobed a spectacular magnification of the spookiness across the street. Shawn and Steve sat huddled in the gazebo, staring intensely at the windows on the rounded spire, and the ones just beneath the steeply-pitched roof. But tonight, just like every other night they had repeated this vigil, those windows revealed nothing but total obscurity.

"What do you think we'll really find in there?" Shawn pondered on his imagination of the mysterious chronicle locked up within the walls of the abandoned structure.

"Hard to say," Steve replied. "Probably a lot of old junk. But just remember... we're not going to take anything. We're just going to look."

"Wouldn't it be great to find some proof?"

"Proof of what?"

"That the ghosts are really there."

"Only one problem with that... how would we ever explain to anyone *how* we discovered it?"

"Good point. Maybe when I'm old and gray I'll write a book about it."

"Yeah. You can call it "Face to Face With the Ghosts of Westland.""

Shawn wasn't quite sure he wanted to come face to

face with someone who had been dead since 1947, but the thought of such an experience was rather entertaining. Scary, but entertaining.

The rain stopped as the thunderheads tumbled off into the northeast, unveiling a crescent moon and twinkling stars playing peek-a-boo among the sporadic, feathery clouds whisking frantically across the black sky. Long, black shadows cast by the lofty oak trees and the huge, eerie house engulfed the back yard all the way to the railroad tracks and beyond. A symphony of cicadas and croaking bullfrogs, accompanied by the whooshing sound of car and truck tires rolling over the rain-drenched Main Street serenaded the night. The storm was over. The thunder was only a distant echo. The third story windows across the street were dark and empty.

The moment Shawn and Steve awaited was at hand. Most of the town was asleep. This was their perfect opportunity.

TWO

Like two cat burglars right out of a bad movie, they hustled into the shadows at the railroad bed. Their black khakis and t-shirts offered little visual exposure from more than twenty feet away. Paranoia sank its teeth into Shawn. Whispering in algebra class was the most serious offense he had ever been *caught* at. But Steve's boldness was giving him a little added confidence, and he was quite determined to satisfy his curiosity.

Armed with crow bar, flashlights, and two intrepid spirits, they scrambled over the fence. Steve led the way through the brambles, following the same path he had forged just a couple days earlier. They were standing at the threshold of discovery, closer to the scary old building than they ever thought possible. Until now, they had only gazed at the mysterious obscurity from the rose garden shelter across the street. But now, they were about to touch it, and even more incredible, they were going inside it. At last, their imagination was about to translate into reality. And the only obstacle between them and curiosity's satisfaction were a few weather-beaten boards that the pry bar would quickly and easily dislodge.

There was still time to abort the mission. If they didn't make the intended use of the crow bar, they wouldn't have committed any invasive aggression other than trampling down a few weeds. But somehow this didn't seem like an unlawful act; it felt more like a defiant child challenging a parental rule. This was a mission of discovery. They *couldn't* turn back now, and after all, how much harm could they possibly do?

Steve put the crow bar into action, and half of the portal was quickly laid open. Their flashlights revealed yet another wooden door recessed into the rock foundation wall. That one swung open with ease, exposing the dark, damp, stale-smelling, dirt-floored dungeon. Never had Steve or Shawn stepped so cautiously, while their lights busily scanned the mostly empty space. Only a couple of wood-staved barrels and several old trunks sat in a corner. There were thick, rock walls separating the cellar into rooms, but they were there more for support of the huge structure above than they were intended as partitions. As Shawn peeked around the end of one of the walls, his light found a steep, ladder-like stairway that led up to a rectangular opening in the ceiling.

At the top of the ladder was another trap door. The hinges rendered an eerie, screeching moan as Steve pushed the door open and ascended into a small, windowless room. Shawn wasn't about to be left alone, and was instantly at Steve's side, standing in what appeared to be a pantry, adjacent to the kitchen, and they knew they were at the rear side of the house by the boarded-up window they could see through the doorway. Gingerly they stepped out of the pantry and into the kitchen, wondering if they would be greeted by the ghosts of Lizzy and Emma Hawthorne. But there was not a sound, or even a hint of motion anywhere.

Under a crusty blanket of dust and a thicket of cobwebs, it was obvious no cuisine had been served up from this kitchen in many years. Rust was consuming the cast iron cook stove, as well as the tin pots and pans on the cupboard shelves. A calendar hanging on one wall still proclaimed the preservation of the last known habitation: July, 1947.

An archway was distinctly the passage into the next room, which was no more than a short, wide corridor, its walls lined with shelves from floor to ceiling, and every one packed end to end with books. So much dust, soot, and mildew covered the spines it was impossible to interpret any of the titles. Shawn's temptation to pull some of them off the shelf for closer inspection was difficult to resist, but he recalled the oath they agreed to before the invasion, *"not to touch or disturb anything inside the house."* Perhaps another time he would have the opportunity to peruse the archaic library, but not tonight.

Yellowed, moth-eaten lace curtains dangled across the filthy window panes that permitted little or no inward vision, but they did allow the luminescence of the street lamps to dimly light the interior of the front parlor. Shawn and Steve switched off their flashlights as they entered. As if stepping into another world, the grandeur of past extravagance was almost breath-taking. If one could overlook the dust and the cobwebs, ignore the peeling and sagging of the once exquisite rose-colored floral wall paper, and disregard the tarnish on the many brass and silver adornments, the imagination could almost bring the past back to life.

Steve walked cautiously to the center of the room among this realm of antiquity. The air was musty-smelling and deathly quiet. As if time had stood still for the past twenty years, the inside of the house looked as though it had not been disturbed in all that time. Everything was left just as it was in 1947: the upright player piano, the hurricane oil lamps, the elaborate crystal chandelier, the huge oak dining table, the Boston rockers next to the rusty pot belly stove—like they were waiting for someone to return after a long vacation.

Shawn aimed his flashlight at some framed pictures gracing the wall to get a better look. In the dim light it was impossible to make out any of them, but Shawn was compelled to see.

"Shawn!" Steve whispered, as if anyone else was there to hear him. "Aren't you afraid someone out there will see that light?"

Shawn already had the situation sized up. "Take a look at those windows. They're so dirty it's no wonder we've never seen anything from out there. And no one is going to see us, either... *and why are you whispering?*"

Steve gazed at the windows. They *were* quite dirty. He could barely see the cars passing on Main Street.

As Shawn made his way around the room eyeing each piece of art, he recognized many of them from the American Literature class he had just aced. Nearly all were signed *Currier and Ives* prints. But the last one he came to sent a chill down Shawn's spine. He beckoned Steve to take a look. The brown-tinted daguerreotype was of two not-so-attractive women in flowing white gowns with leg-of-mutton sleeves. Their piercing glare seemed almost inhuman.

"Do you suppose these are our two ghosts?" Shawn was certain the picture was of Emma and Lizzy Hawthorne.

Steve stared at the photograph for a few seconds. "Man! They *were ugly.*"

Hidden from their view before, they were now standing at the foot of a stairway leading up into the mysterious darkness of the second floor. But who would go first? Side by side, with each squeaky step, they focused on the black hole at the top of the stairs. As they approached the top, their flashlight beams began to reveal their position, and exposed a familiar fixture. They were at the south end of the building; to their right was the interior of the rounded tower at the front corner facing the park. But what was this regulation-sized billiard table doing *here*?

Their attention converged on the spire windows. They realized their dangerously close proximity and quickly doused their lights. With due precautions, slowly and deliberately they crept each to one side of the opening and peeked around the edge of the sill to the street below, just as Jake, the City Police Chief was passing by in the squad car. The powerful cowl-mounted spotlight was scanning the empty park across the street. He certainly hadn't noticed the presence of human form in the second story windows on *this side* of the street. If he had, he was ignoring it completely. The police car continued its slow pace down the road and disappeared out of sight.

The two stood there for a few minutes enjoying the bird's eye view of the city, commenting that "the view from the *third floor* would be even better." But first, they had a *pool table* to examine, and the remainder of the second level to explore.

And a fine table it was. Better than they had ever seen. The coin-operated, six-foot versions at the Bowling Alley couldn't compare to the quality and craftsmanship of this one. It was built of solid mahogany. The slate playing surface was covered with the traditional green felt, but the rails were leather, and all the pockets were *real leather, not plastic.*

Shawn finally violated the oath. He plucked several balls from a corner pocket. "What's this? All the balls are red. How can you play pool when all the balls are the same color?"

Steve chuckled. "Snooker." He knew the game, but hadn't played it much. "There are fifteen red balls, and if you check the side pockets, you'll probably find six colored ones."

Shawn had to look. Sure enough, six various colors, and numbered one through six.

Steve continued with his brief synopsis. "I don't remember all the rules, but you hafta sink a red ball and then you can shoot at the numbered balls, in numerical order, and sink them *only* in the side pockets, so you gotta be good at bank shots. You keep score with points for the numbered balls you get in."

Shawn seemed a little baffled. "Okay, *Snooker Man…* but what were a couple of little old ladies doing with a pool table… *upstairs*?"

Steve shrugged his shoulders. "Guess they didn't have room for it downstairs in the parlor."

It was time to move on. Looking down the long, narrow hallway running the entire length of the house, they could see one doorway on the left, and two on the right. All three rooms were furnished much the same: large brass beds with feather-filled mattresses, corner chairs, round-topped steamer trunks, ball-footed tables, oil lamps, and pastel-colored chamber sets. At the far end of the corridor, they found the staircase to the *third* story. Although this was where the Hawthorne ghosts were always spotted, by now, bold curiosity by far surpassed trepidation as Shawn and Steve ascended these steps with ardent expectations. This was to be the pinnacle of the quest; if anything sensational remained to be discovered, it would be there on the infamous *third* floor.

The possibility of an actual encounter with supernatural entities still lurked in their subconscious, and the closer they came to that last step, the boldness began to melt away. But unwilling to yield to the gripping suspense of what awaited them, they pressed on, slowly.

THREE

The entire third floor was one enormous open room. With their backs toward the wall facing the street, Steve and Shawn made a hasty scan of the vast space. There were no windows to the back or either end, and the walls had no covering—just bare, unfinished boards. It had the appearance of any typical dreary attic. But there was furniture, graceful and ornate, neatly arranged as if this had once been a primary dwelling. Except for the player piano and the rosy wall paper, this was almost a duplicate copy of the downstairs parlor. The pot belly stove was of a smaller version, and there was no chandelier, and the dining table wasn't quite so large, but everything else was nearly the same. And beyond all this, toward the back wall stood two brass beds with thick, soft-looking mattresses, a night table between them, and chamber pots on either side.

But why was it so dark? Why weren't the street lamps casting at least a little light into the room? It became clearly understandable as they turned to investigate the front windows. It was also understandable why they could not have seen anything, *living or otherwise,* in these windows from their spot in the park. Dark-colored, opaque canvass-like fabric draped each one, allowing not even an infinitesimal sliver of illumination to trickle in. If no light was getting in, then no light would pass outward, either. Steve experimented holding the curtain to one side. A flood of light poured in. Replacing it snuffed the room into total darkness again.

"I think it might be safe to light some of these candles. No one outside will see them, and we'll be able to take a better look around."

Shawn gave it some thought, and concluded it seemed to be a good idea. "You got any matches?"

By the time Shawn had voiced his approval, Steve already had one candle lit. It was short and fat and its own solidified pool of drippings had it securely stuck to the bottom of a round-handled tin cup. Its flame emitted an eerie, flickering yellow radiance that sent a giant shadow of Steve's silhouette dancing on the wall behind him. There were half-burned candles everywhere. Within minutes they had most of the chamber well-lit, and now it all seemed to be in a little better perspective. But just like the rest of the house, this room had not been host to any mortal stir for quite some time, either, as dust and cobwebs dominated the decor. There was hardly any clutter, and it did seem odd there were no remnants left behind of a past generation, no discarded or forgotten personal possessions that might help consummate the saga of the Hawthornes, or at least cast a little understanding of the lifestyle exercised by the dwellers here so long ago. Shawn kept hoping to find, perhaps, a diary, or a journal, or *some* recorded memoirs, as he forced open each less-than-cooperative drawer of the old mahogany desk. But the compartments produced little of anything—a couple of quill pens, a dried-out ink well, and three unused candles.

Under the usual layer of dust, in a corner beside a Boston rocker, a small stack of newspapers aroused Steve's attention. They were yellowed and brittle with age. He plucked the top one from the stack, shook away the dust, and read the bold headline:

SOVIETS LAUNCH SPUTNIK II

It was a copy of the *State Journal* dated Monday, November 4, 1957. And the next one especially caught his eye. The bolder-than-bold inscription at the top of the front page jumped out:

BRAVO, BRAVES
MILWAUKEE GOES WILD

He scanned the first few lines of the epitaph from Friday, October 11, 1957, characterizing that city's reaction to their baseball team's glorious success in the World Series.

"Shawn! Come here. Look at this."

At first glance Shawn exhibited an air of disappointment. "They're just some old newspapers." He didn't immediately recognize the gravity of Steve's find.

"Look at the dates," Steve urged. "Notice anything strange about them?"

Shawn picked up the remaining two editions from the floor and began to read aloud the headlines and dates. "Reds Launch First Artificial Satellite, Saturday, October fifth, nineteen fifty-seven." He flipped to the second paper he was holding. "Braves Do It. Aaron's Homer in the Eleventh Wins Pennant, Tuesday, September twenty-fourth, nineteen fifty-seven." Then it hit him. "NINETEEN FIFTY-SEVEN!"

"Exactly," Steve confirmed. "If the Hawthorne twins died in *1947*, and if it's true no one lived here after that, then how did these papers get here?"

Someone had been in the house a decade *after* the Hawthorne double demise. The papers were testimony to that. Had the long-departed siblings re-visited their earthly domain? Or, was there some other explanation yet to be uncovered? This *was* justification enough to suspend the oath and to mount an intensified probe. Not a single corner, nook, or cranny was to go unscrutinized; if there was anything else to find, they were going to find it.

After nearly the entire expanse had been searched inch by inch, nothing more than a few pieces of worthless jewelry had been found. Shawn was standing on a short stool investigating the top shelves of an empty cupboard when he noticed Steve tugging open the drawers of the desk. "I've already looked in there. Didn't find anything."

"But did you pull out the false bottom in the lower drawer on the right?"

"What false bottom?" Shawn almost fell off the stool as he responded to Steve's inquiry.

Steve's sharp eye had noticed that the interior of this drawer was not as deep as the outside, and the exposed bottom seemed to be loose. He pulled a jackknife out of his pocket, stabbed the pointed blade into the soft wood, and carefully lifted out the facade. There, in the hidden compartment, was a two-inch-deep, eight-inch-square cedar box with tarnished brass corners and hinges. Steve hoisted it up onto the desktop. It was heavy. Shawn watched with enthusiastic eyes. They cautiously lifted the hinged top, as if they expected a spring-loaded boxing glove to come flying out. Shawn's heightened anticipation dropped like a rock off a cliff. The box was filled with coins. Just coins. His intellect was expecting something else.

But Steve realized they had uncovered something more than just a batch of loose change. He recognized some of the pieces as similar coinage he had once seen under lock and key at a museum. He positioned a couple of lit candles for better light, and began removing the coins, inspecting them one by one. They weren't the typical, familiar nickels, dimes, and quarters that would be dropped into the slot of a 1965 candy bar vending machine, or plunked down on the counter in exchange for a banana spit at the drug store soda fountain. There were gold twenty- dollar double eagles, ten-dollar eagles, gold dollars, silver dollars, tiny half dimes, bronze two-cent pieces, silver three-cent pieces, strange-looking nickels and over-sized pennies. There were many familiar dimes and quarters too, but not one of the coins in the entire lot bore a date later than 1887. Steve studied the last coin from the box with intensity. It was gold, with the head of an Indian princess on one side, and the words "3 Dollars" surrounded by a wreath on the other. He had never seen the likes of it, much less, ever heard of such a denomination used as common legal tender, although it appeared quite authentic. His T-shirt served well as a polishing cloth, and he soon had the face of the coin emitting a glistening golden luster.

Even though the box of coins didn't answer any questions, what an extraordinary bonanza this was. At face value, there had to be at least two hundred dollars, but to a serious collector, they were probably worth ten times that amount. But how could two teenagers ever explain their procurement of such a rare and valuable stash? They'd be sentenced to *Wales Boys' School*, for sure, if the truth ever surfaced. And what about their self-administered oath? On the other hand, *they* were the only ones to know it had been broken, and they couldn't possibly leave this king's ransom behind.

The wooden box would be too cumbersome to

manage, and much too conspicuous, should anyone see them leaving the premises. Thank goodness, pants come with pockets.

The entire house had been explored, and there was probably nothing more to find. All the candles were extinguished with the certainty that not a single spark remained.

They had entered the lodge of a past society almost two hours ago as innocent, curious, adventure-seeking boys. And now, just after midnight, they were leaving as ravaging thieves. But Shawn justified their actions by saying "You can't *steal* something from *ghosts.*" Their daring act warranted a reward, and this was it.

As Steve ducked out of sight descending the cellar ladder, he commented to Shawn. "Y' know? We just saw something no one else in this whole town has ever seen. Too bad we can't tell anyone."

FOUR

The exploration wasn't over; they had just barely begun. Standing shoulder to shoulder at the base of the steps, they shined their flashlight beacons around the forlorn underground cavern, taking note of the stone-walled maze standing before them.

"Which way did we come in?" Shawn had led the way to this spot on the way in, but he wasn't *exactly* sure, right now, which direction would take them back to the exit.

"I think it's this way" Steve said as he headed around the end of one of the barriers. At the far end of that wall was a dead end, but ten feet to the left, their lights found the doorway. Expecting to breathe in some fresh air, Steve pulled open the door, but instead of the stone steps up to the trap door they had pried open, they were staring into a dark hole. The passageway descended with more rock steps that disappeared around a curve. This definitely wasn't the way out, but as long as they were there for the purpose of discovery, they couldn't just walk away.

"It probably just leads to a storm sewer."

"But why would the basement of a house be connected to a storm sewer?"

Shawn recalled a bit of history. "There were hideaways all over Wisconsin for escaped southern slaves during the Civil War. Maybe this is one of them."

The stairs snaked back and forth, as it descended into the cool, damp reaches of the earth. Shawn lost his footing on the wet, slippery steps, and like a bowler picking up a seven-ten split, Steve tumbled down with him. Fortunately, they were near the bottom; the injuries didn't seem too serious. Steve's right knee was bruised, and the underside of Shawn's left forearm was skinned from the awkward landing, but neither was bleeding, and it didn't seem necessary to abandon the mission for such a minor incident. Time would heal their wounds, and they may not ever get another opportunity like this again.

The passageway went on and on, twisting and turning around, under, and over layers of bedrock. As if it had supported frequent travel at one time, the walking surface was smooth and hard-packed, so it was nearly effortless to maintain a brisk pace, just to keep warm in the chilly air. In some places, the corridor opened up wide enough to drive a Mack truck through, and some stretches were barely adequate for Shawn and Steve to walk side-by-side. After walking over an hour, the temperature suddenly seemed to be rising quickly. It was a logical conclusion they were approaching the end of the tunnel, and they would soon be out in the open, warmer air again. About a hundred feet ahead they could see a faint light. As they slowed their pace, suspicious of what might await them there, a startling hum erupted, and a hazy bluish-green glow engulfed them. Stopped in their tracks by bewilderment, they stood there for ten seconds, looking over the walls and ceiling trying to detect the apparatus responsible for the bizarre circumstances. But they saw nothing. Then, like race horses out of the gate, they quickly stepped forward a few feet. The hum stopped and they were standing in total darkness. Their flashlights were dead.

Shawn whispered "What do you suppose that was?" He was too intrigued to be scared.

"I don't know," Steve replied. "But let's get outa here."

Hoping the path was as smooth and clear ahead, as it had been the rest of the way, they cautiously hiked toward the dim illumination.

On the outside, the entrance was encompassed by huge sandstone boulders, completely concealing it from view in any direction. Steve climbed up onto one of them, and Shawn followed. A bright, glowing full moon was the source of the guiding light. But that didn't seem possible. Three hours earlier, when they entered the old house, the moon was just a sliver.

And where had the tunnel taken them? All they could tell was that they were in a valley, with a steep, heavily wooded hillside behind them, and a gurgling stream below the rocks where they sat. They had experienced enough excitement for one night, and as long as they were *supposed* to be on a camping trip, as they often did during the summer, this seemed a likely spot to get comfortable and sleep until sunrise. They'd figure out *where* they were then.

FIVE

In the soft, hazy sunlight that drifted to their campsite through a canopy of oak, maple, and walnut, an angry, chattering red squirrel was obviously upset with the invasion of his territory by the two strangers who had taken up overnight residency beside the creek. He darted about through the branches of the majestic timber, and the scolding ruckus was so noisy, it woke Steve from a sound, comfortable slumber. He sat up, took inventory of his senses, and realized that Shawn who had been asleep beside him was not there now.

"Good morning, Snooker man." Steve heard Shawn's voice, but he didn't see Shawn. Still a little groggy, he rubbed his eyes and looked around some more. His disorientation diminished, and he was slowly making a re-entry into reality.

"I was beginning to wonder if you were ever gonna wake up."

This time, Steve honed in on the voice. Shawn was perched high atop one of the colossal sandstone boulders just behind him. He had awoken a half hour earlier and decided not to disturb his campmate, scaled the huge rock, and was sitting there enjoying the solitude of this splendid utopia.

Steve pulled off his T-shirt, knelt at the edge of the stream with his knees on a flat rock that was partially submerged in the water so clear he could see the sandy creek bottom. He cupped his hands and scooped up a refreshing splash of the cool water onto his face. It felt so good, he did it again. The water seemed so clean; he didn't hesitate to quench his thirst at the same time.

Using the T-shirt as a towel, he wiped his face dry, and joined Shawn on the broad, flat-topped rock. From up there, they had a panoramic view of the bucolic glen. The jutting hillside blocked their sight, but the valley seemed to widen off to the north, and in the other direction, the entire valley disappeared around a bend. A dozen head of cattle grazed contentedly in the lowland meadow, and beyond them, a lavish, green forest covered the abrupt slope on the other side.

"Have you figured out where we are?" Steve was just now beginning to give it some serious thought as he recalled their peculiar arrival.

"Nope." Shawn's eyes followed the placid stream winding across the valley floor, hoping to jog his memory of a recognizable fishing hole. This place *did* seem oddly familiar, but he couldn't make a connection. Perhaps they were just viewing the area from a different angle they had never seen before, and that's why it appeared so alien to them.

Thinking back to the night before, Steve recalled the tumble they had taken on the slippery steps, and he suddenly realized his knee didn't hurt any more. He slid his pant leg up exposing the knee. There was no bruise. Shawn hadn't thought about it until now, but when he inspected his arm that was skinned in the fall, there was no sign of an injury whatsoever. The bulky weight of all those old coins still present in their pockets certainly proved they had not dreamed the previous night's activities, yet, here they were, in a place they couldn't identify, and it was within walking distance from the streets of their own hometown.

As they sat there discussing their options of which direction to start hiking, the sound of some kind of machinery began echoing through the hills. Clink... clink...clink...clink...clink...clink...clink. The sound wasn't familiar. A few seconds later, another noise rang out, acutely overwhelming the first. But this one was recognizable. It was the sound of a circular saw blade singing through a slab of wood. Shawn knew that sound from his Dad's lumber yard.

"I think it's coming from over there." Steve was pointing to where the valley widened behind the sheer bluff.

"Then that's the way we'll go. There's bound to be a road that will take us *somewhere* we know."

The trail led along the banks of the stream for a distance, then turned abruptly uphill into the woods and followed the contour of the hillside. The sound of the screaming saw was getting louder, but the dense forest kept the source out of their sight. After crossing a broad ravine, the terrain took them to a slightly higher elevation, and just barely visible through the trees, they could see the roof of a building. As they neared the edge of the tree line, the establishment came into plain view, and in the silence between the passes of the saw, they could hear voices, and what sounded like a waterfall.

The unpainted, wood-framed structure stood on a high bank next to the stream, and just behind it was a large pond, as if the water had been dammed. A fifteen-foot-high water wheel was spinning at a remarkable speed as a channel of water fed from the surface of the pond poured onto the top of it. Below the wheel, the water dumped out into another pool, where it re-joined the natural flow of the creek.

Along side the building, opposite the pond, hundreds of huge logs lay scattered about. Four men were rolling one of the logs onto a ramp leading into a large opening in one side of the shed-like structure, while two others were stacking freshly cut boards on a four-wheeled wagon.

Shawn wanted to get a closer look. He led the way as they sauntered down the gradual slope to a more broadside view of the mill. But what they saw as they approached the front of the building stopped them dead in their tracks, speechless. Above the door, in bold black letters, they read the hand-painted sign: KELLY LOGGING & LUMBER CO.

Shawn had seen the old photographs of his grandfather's sawmill in Jasper Valley—the sawmill that his great grandfather built—the sawmill that evolved through three generations of Kelly proprietorship into the prosperous business now occupying a half block of prime real-estate on Main Street. And this was a pretty good replica. But why hadn't he ever heard any mention of the reproduction? And why didn't he know about this place that looked so much like Jasper Valley?

As they scanned the surrounding hills, and gazed up the winding ravine leading away from the mill, Shawn and Steve began to recognize the geographical exactness this valley bore to resemble their beloved recreational getaway. It didn't seem possible, *but this was Jasper Valley*. Without the dam. Without the lake.

In the past, raging springtime floods came gushing down this canyon, threatening, destroying, and sometimes killing. There was no defense, in those days, against the fury and devastation when the floodwaters swallowed up everything in its path, and unrelentingly forced hundreds of inhabitants to seek higher ground, leaving behind their homes and farms to be buried in muck, or even swept away.

Then, in 1957, the construction began, and two years later the Jasper Valley Dam put an end to the terror. The mighty earthen barrier formed a basin capable of containing the worst deluge, and by 1961, a calm and mellow fifty acre lake nestled between the bluffs that granted a matchless rustic seclusion from the rest of the world.

"You boys lookin' fer work?" The grizzly-looking

character startled Shawn and Steve as they gawked at the small clearing where a paved parking lot *should* be. They hadn't noticed him approaching. He was a giant of a man with a voice to match, dressed in faded, worn bib overalls and a shirt badly in need of a trip to the laundry room. A brown straw hat shaded his unshaven face that wasn't smiling as he looked the boys up and down.

"N-no... we're just passing by... heading back to town." Intimidated by the big man, Shawn was reluctant to say any more.

"Well, okay... but if you change your mind, we sure could use a couple more hands out here. Just go talk to Mr. Kelly. You'll find him at the railroad yard in Westland. Tell him 'John' sent ya. He'll put ya to work first thing tomorrow."

"Okay, John... we'll think about it." Steve tugged at Shawn's shirt sleeve as he responded to John's instructions. He was urging Shawn to make a graceful exit, and he certainly wasn't interested in rolling logs or stacking boards.

Confused—and maybe a bit frightened—Shawn stopped midway up the ravine. "This is all just too weird. That guy just told us to go see my Dad for a job. Why hasn't Dad ever told me about the mill? And where the hell is the lake? And where the hell is the road? It should be RIGHT HERE!" A bit of hysteria was creeping into his speech.

Steve put his ever-comforting hand on Shawn's

shoulder, who definitely needed some calming down. "Hey! Settle down, okay? I'm sure there's a logical explanation for all this, and we're going to get it. Now let's get hiking back to town so we can find out what's going on."

They followed the dirt wagon trail as it wound through the rolling countryside around corn fields and small patches of woodland, up toward the ridge where Highway 28 would be buzzing with traffic. With feelings like being lost in a foreign land, they tried to deter their thoughts of the inexplicable predicament by talking about some of their favorite topics, but it was difficult to ignore the surroundings that had so drastically changed in such a short time. It was only a hundred yards to the familiar railroad grade. At last. Something that hadn't changed—something that was still as they knew it.

SIX

The pounding hooves of four chestnut drays pulling a wagon loaded down with the neatly stacked, rough-sawed lumber from the mysterious mill slowed, and came to rest as the driver pressed his foot against the brake lever, pulled back on the reigns, and spoke to his obedient team in a deep, gentle, commanding voice: "Whoooa, Gypsy, whoa." When he was certain the beasts were stilled, he turned to Shawn and Steve. "This here load's goin' to the railroad yard in town fer curin.' Climb up on back... you can ride the rest of the way... that is, if you're goin' to Westland."

It wasn't exactly the ride they were expecting, but *this* encounter with John didn't seem quite so intimidating, and it *was* a long walk into town. So they graciously embraced the offer and scrambled aboard. John talked to the four powerful animals as if he were talking to his children, and with a jerky start, the load was soon rolling at speed again. Not only was he a sawyer, he was a skillful teamster, too.

As the horses cautiously stepped over the train tracks, John expertly guided the huge, wooden-spoked wagon wheels up the stone ramps looming the rails. It was a jolting ride for Shawn and Steve sitting atop the lumber, but they weren't concerned about that. Their attention was drawn to Highway 28. There were no cars. There were no trucks. There was *no pavement.* Just a rut-infested, bumpy, dirt road—*if it could be called a road.* The topography looked about right, but this sure wasn't the highway that was here yesterday.

Their eyes were glued in the direction they would soon see the familiar sights of their hometown. Off in the distance, over the treetops, the church steeple came into view, and now they knew it was just a matter of minutes before they would be sitting at the drug store soda fountain sipping a malted milk and plotting the weekend activities. That's where they usually were on Saturday mornings, and today wouldn't be any different, despite the unusual experiences so far.

As the freight wagon jostled along the rough road, Shawn wondered what his father would have to say about the sawmill he had kept a secret all this time. And he wondered where this unknown road would lead into town. The later question was answered quickly. John turned the wagon across the railroad tracks, and down a short grade, and then rumbled over a narrow, plank-topped bridge. A row of catslide houses lined the left side of the road, and a jagged ditch paralleled on the right. He knew where they were, and so did Steve. This was Black Creek Avenue and just ahead it connected to Main Street, a few blocks from downtown Westland.

This *was* Westland, but certainly *not* the city as they

knew it. Many of the building shapes were recognizable, but there was so much missing. The knoll off on the left where the water tower should be was now home to an unpainted wood shack and a flock of chickens. The *Pure Oil* Gas Station was gone, and in place of the big, stately homes that once graced either side of this end of Main Street, was a sparse scattering of shanties and little log cabins.

The unpaved streets were heavily populated with more horses and mules than Steve and Shawn had ever seen in one place—even at the County Fair—hitched to buckboards, buggies, drummers' wagons, and carriages of all shapes and sizes. They sat speechless in awe while they watched their strangely transformed town pass by, and the many unfamiliar faces waving to John as he rolled the lumber load down the street, headed for the railroad yard.

John's gentle but stern command to the leaders broke their trance. "Haw, Gypsy, haw." The wagon slowed and began turning left toward a small shack with stacks of boards and timbers all around it, and next to the driveway was a sign that read "KELLY LOGGING & LUMBER CO." The boys had a suspicion they weren't going to meet Shawn's father here, and decided this was a good place to disembark the transport, before they were confronted by someone they didn't *want* to meet.

This was unbelievable. Not twelve hours ago they had walked this very sidewalk on their way to the park. It was concrete then, but now it was wooden boards they were treading over as they passed by store windows with signs hand-painted on the glass. One read: "COBBLER—BOOTBLACK." Another said "CHANDLER—TALLOWS & LAMPS," and the store they knew as Flander's Hardware displayed a large sign on the front naming it "WESTLAND EMPORIUM." Across the dusty street was the "CLOVER LEAF GENERAL STORE," a barber pole and sign reading "HAIRCUT—10 CENTS," and another small window simply said "SEAMSTRESS."

"Okay... where are all the cameras?" Steve said calmly.

"What cameras?" Shawn asked curiously.

"Well, we must have wondered onto the set for *The Wild, Wild West*... or maybe *Bonanza*."

"That's ridiculous."

"Not any more ridiculous than us standing here in a town that looks more like Dodge City than it does Westland."

Outsiders in their own domicile, they were receiving plenty of curious ogles from the townspeople, so it seemed moving on was in order. Steve suggested they should trek toward the north end of the city; his dad's auto repair shop was there, and his house was next-door. Somewhere, there had to be an answer for all this, and maybe they would find it there.

But "Edgar's Service Garage," where Steve's Dad had been a mechanic for the past fifteen years was nowhere to be seen. Neither was his home. Instead of the expected modern, steel structure was a wood-framed barn-like building, and on the front was lettered "GARETT'S BLACKSMITH AND LIVERY," and it, too, was surrounded by more equines, wagons and carriages.

Perplexed, but not out of ideas, Steve said, "Okay... let's go to the rocks. Rocks don't change and they don't disappear."

The rocks—some as big as houses—were one of their favorite childhood spots for play, and more recently, a place of solitude to where they often retreated for privacy. Hidden away in a grove of lofty oaks and pines at the west boundary of the city, those huge rocks had been the site of many cowboy and Indian encounters. They had seen Shawn and Steve through puberty, and adolescence, and their *initials were chiseled into the face of one big boulder.*

The towering trees they were accustomed to seeing mingled among the rocks were nothing more than saplings and brush. No child's games had been played here, nor were there any inscriptions anywhere. Now the substance of the circumstances was beginning to surface as reality. Suddenly, the works of *Lewis Carroll* and *Jules Verne* didn't seem so far-fetched. There weren't any talking animals, or steaming pools of bubbling lava, but it was strange, nonetheless. Today, the security of *home* had evaporated, as they felt trapped in a pioneer version of the quiet Midwestern community where they grew up. The rocks were the only remnants of familiar recollection, and even this area lacked the comforting tranquility it had once endowed.

Steve climbed up the stair step arrangement of granite to a ledge where they often perched, and Shawn followed. It was a good place to contemplate the predicament, and maybe project a solution.

"I know this sounds crazy..." Shawn was trying not to allow his best friend certify him as a mental case. "But let's consider the facts. The lake is gone; the roads are gone; the water tower is gone; most of Westland is gone. But I don't think all those things *disappeared*. They just haven't been built yet."

"And we've gone back in time to God knows when." Steve was accepting the concept—as impossible as it seemed—that they had transversed an impenetrable barrier in epic proportions.

"As close as I can figure, this is about 1890. My great-grandfather built that sawmill in Jasper Valley in the late 1880s, and that building didn't look that old... if you know what I mean."

"And I remember when the dam was built. We were in the fourth or fifth grade." Steve counted on his fingers. "That would have been about '57 or '58."

"Yeah... Mom and Dad wouldn't let us go out there to watch... they said it was too dangerous... but we snuck out there on our bikes, anyway."

Steve directed the conversation back to the present situation. "But how did this happen? How did we get here... and how are we going to get out of here again?"

Shawn had already been pondering that thought.

"Remember that strange green light in the tunnel last night? When we walked through there is when it happened, and the only way we'll get back to where we belong is to go back through the tunnel."

"What if it doesn't work going the other way?"

"Then I guess we'll have to see John about a job at the sawmill."

By the sun almost directly overhead, they determined it must be about noon, or just a little after. They hadn't eaten anything all day, and they *were* hungry, so it was decided they would find a way to satisfy their appetites before making the trip back to the valley, the tunnel, and hopefully home.

SEVEN

Downtown Westland, today, didn't have much to offer in the way of restaurants—the popular Bergen's Cafe didn't exist yet, and the bakery wasn't there, either. The pool hall was absent, as was the drug store soda fountain.

In front of the General Store, two elderly, gray-bearded, bib-overalled gentlemen sat on a couple nail kegs, elbows on their knees, and intently studying the checkerboard between them on another keg.

"Excuse me... we're new in town and I was wondering if you could tell us where we might get a bite to eat."

The old gents were so engrossed in their game, they didn't even notice the somewhat out-of-place strangers. "The Hotel over yonder has dern good vittles, but jist so ya know, a helpin' o' chicken stew'll cost ya two bits each."

Steve shaded his eyes from the sun with one hand at his forehead, and pointed to the large sign hanging over the boardwalk just down the block across the street. "Much obliged, sir."

As they headed down the street, Shawn looked at Steve with a quizzical grin. *"Much obliged?* What possessed you to say that instead of *thank you?"*

Steve looked straight ahead toward the Hotel and calmly replied, "That's what John Wayne always says in all the westerns."

They walked across the squeaky, bare wood floor of the dining room containing five empty, square tables covered with white linen tablecloths. The walls were lined with the same rose-colored, flowered wall paper as they had seen in the Hawthorne house parlor, and whale oil peg lamps hung from the wall above each table.

A tantalizing aroma of spices, cinnamon mostly, filled the room. It was almost better than the bakery smells they knew from their own time. They pulled the spindle-backed chairs from under the table and sat down just as a heavy-set, middle-aged woman wearing a long, gray and blue calico dress entered from the kitchen.

"You fellers needin' rooms... or are ya here fer the job?"

Steve let his charm pour out. "No, ma'am, we're just powerful hungry. We're here to eat."

"Ya got money?" This princess was not going to win any Miss Congeniality awards any time soon.

"Yes, ma'am... we've got plenty of money."

"Yeah, lookit ya. Fancy store clothes. Guess you ain't

no guttersnipe. Today it's chicken stew... and I s'pose ya can already smell the pan-dowdy... just made it. I'll bring it right out."

They didn't know what pan-dowdy was, but if it tasted as good as it smelled, the day wouldn't be lost. And when they had finished the frontier cuisine, they only wished there was more--it was delicious. They each slipped a half dime and a quarter under their plates, and Steve handed two quarters to the woman. "There you are. Four bits. Is that enough?"

"It sure is, and you fellers come back anytime."

As they strolled out the door, Shawn turned back toward the maid. *"Much obliged, ma'am."*

Out on the street, the horses tied at the hitching posts were jibbing and rearing. They were getting spooked by something. There was a rumbling, and then came two short blasts, one long blast, and another short one. A whistle. A train whistle. People were scurrying to line up alongside the tracks. Rather than the huge diesel locomotives they usually saw rumbling through, Shawn and Steve stood at the front door of the Hotel and watched the not-so-large, black steam engine roll to a squealing stop, billowing a cloud of gray smoke from its stack. In tow behind it were three passenger coaches, a flat car, two box cars, and a caboose.

Like a choreographed ballet, a dozen men and boys began loading and stacking lumber onto the flat, while six others rolled wooden barrels from one of the box cars onto a platform next to the tracks. Passengers filed down the steps at the rear of the coaches and headed to the station house to collect their baggage, and when all were off, departing passengers began boarding. In less than fifteen minutes, the lumber was secured, the box car doors slid shut, and the new passengers were settled in the coaches. The "All Aboard" was yelled out as the conductor leaned off the coach steps waving his arm as a visual signal to the engineer. A silver bell atop the locomotive rang repeatedly as to say "get the hell out of the way—we're rolling." Puffing out even larger quantities of dark smoke, the iron horse slowly started chugging its way out of sight as the spectators waved good-bye to their families and friends on board.

EIGHT

It was a long, hot walk, even taking the short-cut they knew back to the valley under a blistering July sun. The saw was still singing out its mournful cries as the two nomads slipped by along the tree line. They could see John and the others laboring as hard now as they were early that morning. But it was time to put all this behind and not look back. The Nineteenth Century had to stay right where it was, and Shawn and Steve had to return to the security of their own time, to a Westland they knew.

"Our flashlights. They're dead. How are we going to see to get back?" A streak of panic shot through Shawn as he picked up the lights they had left on the rocks at the entrance to the tunnel.

Steve was a little more confident. "The path through there is nice and smooth. We can feel our way along the walls easy enough. We can't get lost. It only goes one way."

After a cool drink from the stream, they built up the courage to start the dreaded, dark journey. They entered the tunnel, leaving behind the setting sun of the past, and in hopes the strange green light would reset the clock to 1965. And they would only know, for sure, when they emerged from the Hawthorne house at the other end.

Just as they expected, the eerie hum commenced and they were soon standing there engulfed in the blue-green haze of the extraordinary phenomenon. And then it stopped. Shawn's flashlight was lit; he had left the switch on. Steve tried his, and that one lit as well. They looked back toward the tunnel entrance. It was dark. Although the one possible escape route appeared to be gone, they thought this was a likely indication they were on their way back home.

Few words were spoken during the brisk walk through the cold passageway, and because they had traveled it once before, it didn't seem as far this time. Recalling the mishap on their last encounter with the wet, slippery stone steps, a little extra caution found them at the top without incident, and at last, they were right back where they started, in the musty cellar seeking the exit among the maze of rock walls.

As they emerged from the broken trap door, the sliver of a crescent moon smiled down at them. They *were* home.

Their *Schwinns*, with sleeping bags lashed to the handlebars, were well-hidden and waiting for them in the bushes behind Edgar's. A refreshing swim in the lake, and a peaceful night's sleep on the beach sounded mighty inviting right now, but not before they took a quick tour of the town, just to make sure everything was where it should be. And it was. The cafe was there. The bakery was there. The pool hall. The drug store. Flander's Hardware, and the water tower. And the giant oak and pine trees once again shadowed the the huge rocks where the initials 'S. K.' and 'S. A.' were carved into them. The distant roar of a diesel truck engine and the hum of eighteen tires sang through the still night like music. It was here. It was *all* here.

At dawn's first light, the two had hardly slept at all. The excitement of such an incredible adventure kept them awake through the night, sitting there on the Jasper Lake beach exchanging comments and observations, ideas and speculations. Their pockets were full of money they couldn't spend, and their heads were full of experiences they couldn't share with anyone else.

As long as they were awake, and the sun was just starting to peek over the treetops, a point of curiosity had to be explored. They were quite certain they would find nothing, but a search of the hill along the near side of the lake would satisfy their need to know that the tunnel, at least this end of it, no longer existed. They walked the shore of the lake all the way to the top of the dam, and far beyond. The terrain had all changed since *yesterday* as the excavation had altered the contour, and water now covered the creek bank where they had slept the night before. Standing at the crest of the enormous dam, they knew that buried deep beneath it was the mouth of the underground passage.

The excursion had begun on Friday night. All day Saturday had been spent in the *other* Westland, and for all practical purposes, to Shawn and Steve, this was Sunday. But they were in for one more unexpected discovery. As they rolled their two-wheelers into downtown Westland, it didn't seem like a Sunday at all. The stores were open and conducting business; Main Street was alive with activity. Even the bank had customers coming and going. This certainly couldn't be Sunday.

"There's my usual Saturday morning malted milk connoisseurs. What'll it be today?" Otis asked as they swung open the drugstore door and took their regular stools at the soda fountain counter. Otis Ramsey operated the pharmacy/soda fountain/gift shop establishment for as long as Steve and Shawn could remember, and he concocted the thickest, tastiest malteds this side of the Rocky Mountains. He could almost set his clock by the ritual visits Shawn and Steve made to his ice cream parlor every Saturday morning since they were knee-high to a milk stool.

Otis didn't truly understand the actual reason Shawn asked "Is this really Saturday?"

As if it were just normal chit-chat, he replied "Yup... all day, if it doesn't rain."

"I'll have black cherry."

"Okay... and how about you, Steve?"

"Make mine the same... and can we get them to go?"

Steve knew they couldn't talk there, and he was anxious to discuss the time anomaly. The rocks would lend a more confidential backdrop.

The dialogue inspired by their recent encounter endured much longer than the black cherry malts. Now there was a lot more to analyze. They began to realize there was more to this than they first thought, and the longer they talked, the more intrigued they were with pursuing the strange happening. Even though they had spent a whole day at the other end of the tunnel, they returned from the excursion at the same time they had left, and that opened up some speculative possibilities.

"Let's go back there again." Steve was thoroughly convinced it would be safe. They hadn't learned a single thing about the Hawthorne legend, which had been their primary goal. And they wouldn't be missing out on any of their planned summertime activities—not a single minute.

Although Shawn had deeper roots in that quantum time zone, he had reservations about making a second journey into it. The possibility of learning something of his ancestry contrary to the admirable tales he grew up with frightened him, and he wasn't too eager to come face to face with his long-deceased great grandfather. And they already experienced one close call like that when Gypsy nosed the lumber wagon into the railroad yard.

Steve was persistent. "But if we're careful, we don't have to take that chance... and if we go prepared, we can stay as long as we want. When we come back, it'll still be the same time as when we left. We've got plenty of money to use there. If dinner only costs a quarter, with what we've got we could survive a lifetime. I can't think of a better way to go on vacation, and I can't think of a good reason *not to go*. What'ya say? Let's do it."

After he gave it some thought, Shawn realized it was a monumental opportunity, but apprehension took precedence over impulse, and he insisted they take plenty of time to prepare adequately for the expedition. A trip to the Public Library seemed necessary, if for no other reason, to learn the meaning of the term "guttersnipe," and why he had nearly been mistaken as being one. If they were going to venture off into a strange land, they at least should learn the language.

NINE

A leap into the fourth dimension might seem like an immeasurable undertaking, even to the most resolute physicist. The theory of a parallel universe actually existing, or another era occupying our biosphere, was just that—theory. To everyone except Shawn Kelly and Steve Allison. But they weren't considering the experience as a scientific break-through that could alter modern man's course of existence. To them, it was an oracle to warden with diligence, for this was the fruit of the many miserable, wet, discouraging nights they had endured in the park shelter, and revealing the secret to anyone else could very well deprive them of relishing the payoff, not to mention that it might land them in the psyche ward. Without a doubt, they would be labed "certifiably loony" if the public got wind of their claim.

Shawn was a notable scholar, so it didn't seem unusual for him to visit the Public Library, even during summer vacation, to feed his omnivorous hunger for knowledge. Sara Fremont, the gray-haired, pixy-faced librarian had grown to know Shawn well over the past few years as he was the one regular juvenile patron she considered her favorite of all the youngsters to pass through the library doors. They shared a commendable alliance, despite the decades of age difference, as together they had superbly spanned the generation gap utilizing books as their building blocks and compatible personalities as the planks between them.

Sara didn't question Shawn's interest in Nineteenth Century trivia, although she was a bit curious of how he had acquired the need to know that era's usage of the term *guttersnipe*. And as Shawn sat quietly, paging through a stack of publications, Sara proudly announced she had located a passage to answer his query, and began reading aloud to him. "It says here that *guttersnipe* was the name given to homeless children, generally orphaned by accidents, illness and savage native attacks. These children roamed and slept in the streets of the cities..."

"Much obliged, Miss Sara." Shawn was practicing the *new language*. He wasn't going to volunteer a reason for wanting to know, and he desperately hoped she wouldn't ask.

Busy all week with odd jobs and chores around the house and at his Dad's garage, Steve didn't join his adventure companion at the library until Thursday evening. But he did a pretty good job of catch up, and later that night, Shawn filled in all the blanks the best he could.

"Hats," Shawn explained. "That's why people were staring at us so much. We weren't wearing hats. You remember seeing anyone there who didn't have on a hat? One book I read said that in those days people considered themselves only half-dressed if they left home without a hat. And blue jeans were called *Kentucky Jeans* and *Levis* have been around since 1850."

Shawn went on for an hour passing as much of the new-found wisdom to Steve as he could remember, and both hoped they had enough information of the time they were about to visit to be able to blend into that society without being too conspicuous. They knew how they would have to dress, and they would recognize many of the terms and expressions in speech, and hopefully, they were well-versed enough with the customs to know how to act if confronted with social endeavors.

Friday night, once again, seemed to be the most appropriate time to begin the journey, but this time they would take with them a few survival items, just in case something went awry, or, if for some reason, the convenience of the General Store became inaccessible. But they would have to be careful in selecting the proper gear. Suspicions would certainly arise by the sight of a nylon pup tent in 1890, so a light-weight portion of canvas and some clothes line rope could suffice as shelter, if need be. Two blankets, a wooden-handled hatchet and a keenly sharpened hunting knife were a must, and a couple of cans of pork and beans, and a pound, or so, of beef jerky would get them by in a pinch. Two extra pairs of socks and long-sleeved flannel shirts for each rounded out the supply list, and all this had to fit into a couple of pillow case-sized denim laundry bags.

All in all, this didn't seem much different from any other camping excursion they had planned, with the exception of *where* they were headed. They were going so far, yet, so near, and although they were barely leaving their own back yards, they knew little of what to expect. The first sojourn had merely given them a teasing taste, and now they were confident they were ready for the main course. The risk of getting trapped in a time where they didn't belong, or combating the many potential dangers they might face, were of little concern to the two dauntless explorers as they shrewdly continued their preparations to turn back the clock—*and the calendar.*

As the sun was going down that evening, Shawn and Steve, clad in plain, gray T-shirts, faded, worn *Levis*, pockets bulging with the bulk of the old coins, work boots, and a couple of old straw hats they found in the Kelly garage loft, sat in the park shelter patiently awaiting the cover of darkness. Now, the sight of the withered old house didn't seem so frightening, but rather, enticingly appealing.

The previous forced entry had not been discovered. The cellar door's loosened hinges were just as they had left them a week ago, so the access this time was effortless and swift.

TEN

They had definitely returned to the same place. The valley was just as serene and picturesque now as it was on the first visit, and this time, *two* fat red squirrels scolded the intrusion. The creek was still fresh and clean, and the sweet aroma of wildflowers drifted along with the gentle breeze. And just as before, the cry of the saw blade echoed between the hills.

But the sawmill wasn't the same as they had last seen it. Now, there were numerous stacks of sawed lumber, many more logs than before, and another building had been erected, and both it and the mill were painted gray. The operation had broadened, and the changes warranted some scrutiny, but this time from the cover of the woods, as Shawn was still a little skittish about getting too close and being discovered.

There was plenty of time, so a leisurely walk into town with frequent rest stops along the way took most of the morning hours. The arrival back in Westland unveiled more alterations of the town they saw previously. There seemed to be a few more buildings at the town's center, some of the storefront signs had changed, and even some of the trees seemed taller. Quite unlikely, this was just a week later than the first visit. In no way could all these changes and additions been accomplished in a week's time.

"Hey! I 'member you boys... you were here once last

summer." The big voice startled Shawn and Steve, just as it had a week ago at the mill. John Aderly came out of the General Store as if he was on a mission. He recognized the boys and paused only long enough to make his acknowledgment of their presence. Then he proceeded across the street where Gypsy and company, hitched to the empty *Owensboro* freight wagon stood poised and ready for the return trip to the valley sawmill.

"Well," Steve said. "Guess that answers that question. It's a year later than last week."

Some things hadn't changed, though. Horses and mules *still* appeared to be the principal mode of transportation over the *still* dirt roads and streets. Hats were still *the* fashion statement, and the smoke-belching black steam locomotive still rumbled to a squealing stop at mid-day. Kelly Lumber Company still did a land office business, and gray-haired, old gentlemen still played checkers on nail kegs in front of the General Store. And the Hotel still served a mighty fine plateful of chicken stew and apple pan-dowdy for twenty-five cents.

Although several cabins had now been constructed fairly close by, the rocks seemed to be yet untouched, and their seclusion was the perfect spot to stash the tote bags while more exploration was carried out. This might even be where they would call *home* for a while should the stay get lengthy. Behind those rocks, their campsite would be obscure, and sheltered, and this was the only remaining *familiar* piece of real-estate that assured Shawn and Steve they were still on home turf.

They already knew what preceded Steve's digs, and his Dad's workplace, so it seemed fitting to make the mile hike west to investigate the beginnings of the Kelly homestead. No more than another dirt wagon trail zigzagged around the fields across the rolling prairie land, a far cry from the straight graveled roadway that would someday cut its path through the countryside.

They stood on a knoll among the knee-high corn gazing toward a virgin meadow where a half dozen Guernsey cows dined on the succulent grass. A hundred yards beyond, white smoke curled into the air from a stone chimney hugging the outside wall of a modest log cabin, and a small barn authoritatively punctuated the vast space.

"How about that, Shawn? You live in a pasture."

"Yeah... well at least I know now what that old rock foundation in the field behind our house is. As small as it is, I'd never have guessed that it was somebody's house."

Off to their right, partially hidden in a grove of pines and cedars, they could see another structure that couldn't be left uninvestigated. This was the location where Shawn had spent a great deal of time when he was a little boy. The tiny, salt box building certainly wasn't the same, but the name above the door sure was: Underwood School. Until its closing in 1957, Shawn had attended his first three years of elementary school right here at Underwood. Now he was beginning to feel a greater sense of connection with the unusual surroundings.

But on the edge of town, not even a rudimental version of Westland High existed. The campus now consisted of another log house, a barn, three haystacks, a corral, and a huge vegetable garden. The football field was a marsh, and the baseball diamond was a pumpkin patch.

The stories they had heard about the Public Library once being the Town Marshall's Office were now confirmed accurate. And although the cosmetics of the entire downtown area were somewhat different now, *this* Westland was starting to feel more like home. Life seemed uncomplicated here, and if they only had homes to go to, what a great place and time this would be.

Beyond the business district to the south, atop the highest plot of ground in the city, the familiar majestic church steeple towered above the trees, a silent sentry guarding the provincial neighborhood. It seemed to lure Shawn and Steve nearer as the sun settled lower and lower into the western sky. As they walked toward it, they realized this part of their town was less like the Westland they knew. Little development had occurred here yet; where the city park should be, the land was still covered with trees and brush, with a single wagon trail cleared through it leading past the church, over the hill and out onto the open plain. It was hard to imagine the steps of progress that must have taken place to transform this jungle into the active South Main Street where Kelly Lumber Company, the feed mill, the creamery, several warehouses, and scores of homes would eventually rise up.

Only one house and a carriage barn occupied a clearing in the woodland about half way between downtown and the church. It was a grand frontier fortress, proclaiming a certain elegance that seemed misplaced in the proximity of an otherwise rustic settlement. The Romanesque architecture, the gleaming white paint, the sparkling windows, all suggested wealth and success, and would be more appropriately situated on a Southern cotton plantation than here.

Nearly unperceivable in its aboriginal state, Shawn and Steve stared at the noble mansion from the wagon path. Hauntingly familiar to them, the house suddenly took its place in actuality: the shape was right, the placement was right. There was no doubt. *This was the Hawthorne house.* Not the dilapidated old wreck they had always known; not the spooky, lifeless structure that everyone in 1965 shunned; not the eyesore that many hoped would soon be demolished and forgotten. Rather, it was an eloquent statement of beauty and charm, that, if seen in 1965 would be deserving of notice and reverence, and not the prime target for the demolition wrecking ball.

Across the road, well within the cover of box elder and sumac, Shawn and Steve ducked out of sight to a spot they concluded must be nearly the precise location of the future rose garden gazebo, where in all reality this fantastic journey had begun. There were signs of a previous campsite here: a heap of ashes encircled by a ring of stones, and a couple of logs positioned near by as makeshift seating. And the Hawthorne house was in plain view across the road. There was enough daylight left to retrieve their gear from the rocks and return to the new found retreat. They couldn't pass up this opportunity to observe first hand the origin of a legend.

The clothes line rope tightly tied waist-high between two trees and the canvas tarp stretched over it and staked to the ground at the ends was the best shelter they would have for the time being. It would at least keep the dew off their blankets, and barring any hard rain they should be able to stay dry. Steve went in search with the hatchet for a few dry branches, anticipating the desire for a small campfire later on. But when he returned with the armful of firewood, he realized one important commodity had been overlooked when they were packing the supplies.

"Matches," he said in a disgusted tone. "We forgot to bring matches. Guess we won't have a fire tonight."

"That's okay," Shawn said as he dug to the bottom of one of the denim bags. "We can get some at the General Store tomorrow." He pulled out a pair of small binoculars. "But I'm glad I remembered these."

Steve wasn't aware the binoculars had been packed, and expressed he would have rather preferred the matches. But binoculars seemed to be a pretty good idea, too. They would certainly come in handy now.

The tent was fabricated, the unusable firewood was

gathered. For all practical purposes, they were settled in as well as they could expect, considering. And although they might have favored a hot, steaming pizza, a can of cold pork and beans and some beef jerky really hit the spot. After all, they *were* camping.

The brightly painted mansion walls across the road were capturing the last rays of the fiery setting sun as it slowly extinguished the day. The horse-and-wagon traffic had diminished earlier, and now it had ceased entirely. The daily stir was coming to a halt. No street lamps would brighten the metropolis tonight, or for many nights to come. No televisions or hi-fis would be heard from open windows. No roaring diesel trucks slicing through the darkness. No adolescent squealing tires piercing the night. Just as plentiful now as in 1965, singing cicadas and frogs accented the stillness. Westland was retiring for the night. Tomorrow would be soon enough to complete the unfinished tasks of today.

ELEVEN

As dusk drew attention to the oil lamps coming to life inside the manor, two figures, one in a pale pink dress, and the other in blue, emerged through the front door, stood together on the porch for a short time, then descended the steps and strolled toward town. As Steve peered at the young women through the binoculars, Shawn asked "Is it the Hawthorne twins?"

"No. They're too young... and too pretty." Steve recalled the photograph hanging in the *old* Hawthorne parlor, and according to the stories, if they were accurate, Emma and Lizzy Hawthorne should be about 43 years old now, if they died at age 100 in 1947. These two appeared to be in their early twenties, quite attractive, with shoulder-length blonde hair. They *definitely* weren't Emma and Lizzy.

As they disappeared out of sight, a third dark-haired girl about the same age, wearing a bright green outfit, and accompanied by a thirty-something gentleman, approached the verandah, and went inside. A few minutes passed, and one of the first pair returned, and not too far behind, the other followed, both arm-in-arm with young men.

Soon after the third couple entered, the honky-tonk sounds of *The Flying Trapeze* began rolling off the player piano, echoing through the forest. Shawn and Steve watched intently as the images of the waltzing pairs seemed to be having a good time. But Shawn was eyeing the lighted third story windows with more intensity than the parlor affair. Those portals were very dimly lit, and just as in his own time, there didn't seem to be any activity there now, either.

Oh My Darling Clementine wasn't exactly the *Beatles* or *The Beach Boys*, but it was a relief from the first tune that had repeated several times. The gala in the parlor continued, and there was still no movement detected on the top floor.

"What ya lookin' at?" That wasn't Shawn's voice. It wasn't Steve's, either. They were so engrossed in the spy session, they hadn't noticed their visitors quietly approach and take up positions just behind them. Startled at first, Shawn and Steve quickly realized these unexpected guests were just a couple of curious kids, and posed no threat. They were friendly and polite, and by now, Steve and Shawn welcomed the contact with other real people, an act they had been avoiding all day.

"Sorry. Didn't mean t' knock ya into a cocked hat like that. Me 'n Brady... we're campin' out by Miller's Pond. We got tired o' fishin'. Weren't catchin' a dad-blamed thing... so we decided to go for a walk. We come here a lot. Didn't 'spect to find other bodies here."

Steve had to quickly invent a reason for his and Shawn's presence. "We're just passin' through. We're from... ah... Saint Louis. We decided to hold up here for a few days... kinda like it here."

"Ya ain't none o' them rowdies, are ya?"

Shawn remembered the term from his research and assured the two fellows that he and Steve were *not* trouble makers, and were no one to be afraid of.

"What ya need here is a fire. How come ya ain't got a fire goin'?"

"Matches," Steve said. "We don't have any matches. Forgot to get some."

The taller boy dug in his pocket. The grin on his face expressed the pleasure he found in helping out the travelers, and within minutes he had a crackling flame curling bluish gray smoke up into the moonlight.

Barefoot, shirtless, and pants held up with suspenders, he threw his straw hat on the ground and sat down beside Steve on one of the logs, as did Shawn and the other boy.

"My name is Spencer Garett. My Pa runs the blacksmith and livery over yonder. And this here is my best friend Brady Pendleton. His Pa cuts trees fer Kelly Loggin'. We ain't got a whole lot o' friends. We don't get along too good with the b'hoys, 'n there ain't no other bodies like us around, so we kinda just stick t'gether most o' th' time.

It wasn't difficult to interpret Spencer's oration. He and Brady had separated themselves from the ruffian society because they didn't fit in with that crowd. They didn't seem to be sissies, by any means, but they weren't macho he-men either, and they knew it. But they didn't seem to be ashamed of it, nor did they try to hide it. Their eagerness to befriend Shawn and Steve was genuine and sincere, and was well received.

Because Brady's father worked for Shawn's great grandfather, it was certain Shawn couldn't divulge his real name. He thought of spawning some alias, but that could create problems later, so he hoped just first names would suffice. "I'm Shawn, and this is *my* best friend, Steve."

They all shook hands like gentlemen, and reclaimed their original seats around the campfire. New alliances had formed instantly, and although Shawn and Steve recognized fifteen-year-old Spencer and fourteen-year-old Brady to be a bit naive, by 1965 standards, and perhaps a little puerile, by *any* standards, they also saw intelligent, alert, and adventurous new friends.

"Miss Ellie Graham, the school marm, says one more winter o' book learnin' 'n we'll be ready t' go out 'n do whatever we wanna do. We're goin' t' Calyforny t' pan fer gold." Brady's English left some room for improvement, as did Spencer's, but they had a plan and a direction in life. Shawn and Steve were beginning to see more and more similarities of themselves in their new acquaintances, and it seemed almost ironic that, in reality, Spencer and Brady had probably already realized their dreams, many years ago.

The conversation turned to the Hawthorne house when Steve realized the piano serenade had stopped. He described the social event he and Shawn witnessed earlier involving the young ladies.

"Ladies!" Spencer exclaimed. "They ain't no ladies. They're whores! And sure as blazes, that ain't no church social." He went on to spell out the *real* circumstances.

In years past, the Hawthorne twins had conned everyone into believing they were poor widows, whose husbands had died a gallant death fighting at General Grant's side during the Civil War. They gained the sympathy of the settlement, and earned a handsome living selling themselves to the men folk on the street. But as they aged, Lizzy and Emma had become somewhat undesirable to their patrons, and now their home was a boarding house for younger, more desirable female prostitutes, for a king's share of the profits. Over the past few years, many girls had come and gone, and the ones presently doing business across the road had been imported from Milwaukee, Boston, and New York.

Spencer seemed to have all the facts. "Fer a Half Eagle, a man can stay fer an hour; fer a Eagle, till midnight; fer a Double Eagle, all night, a bath, and breakfast next sun up."

Now it was clear to Shawn and Steve how the Hawthorne twins had become wealthy enough to afford such an elaborate home, and why they had found the box full of money hidden in the attic. And this epic, coming from an indigenous citizen of the time, suggested more logic than the one of *Salem Witches*, contrived by rumor and imagination of the next century.

Steve wondered how a fifteen-year-old boy could know all this information with any degree of accuracy.

"Have you ever been there?"

"Me? I weren't born in th' woods t' be scared by an owl. I wouldn't go near that place, and if ya know what's good fer ya, if ya ain't invited, ya better keep yer distance, too. Them Hawthornes is evil people. They've lived here fer ever, and if ya never seen 'em, they're ugly as coon dogs."

Brady jumped in with his story, too. "Once, I seen a stray mongrel wander into their yard. He lifted his leg t' piss on th' posies. Lizzy was watchin' in the front winder, and as the hound was pissin', he jist keeled over, dead as a barn pole."

Shawn and Steve were agog with all the colorful language their counterparts were spewing out. This was turning out to be an experience far beyond what they had expected, and somehow, they knew it would get even better.

Shawn wanted to learn more about the town and its people, and what better observations could they get than from these two characters? Spencer and Brady had plenty to tell, and the captivating delivery was more than informative. It was downright entertaining.

They told sagas about George Flagg, the Town Marshall, how last year he single-handedly captured a couple of cattle rustlers out at the Duncan ranch, and how once, he shot a road agent right off his horse, and how he had run off the rowdies from Chicago, and just last month, he locked up a drummer for selling bottles of sugar water he claimed to be some "miracle medicine."

The stories went on about the General Store owner, Floyd Donovan, who must have eyes in the back of his head, and Evan Johnson, the proprietor of the Emporium *and* the best sharp-shooter in Westland. With a '73 Winchester, at fifty yards he could pick a flea off a hen's tail and never ruffle her feathers. Ellie Graham, the school marm at Underwood, had to be the smartest person alive since George Washington.

"And don't be skeered o' ol' Black Wolf. Every Wednesday this ol' Injun comes into town and trades a blanket, or a bead necklace, or sometimes a bone-handled huntin' knife he's made fer a jug o' whiskey at the Gen'ral Store. Floyd's the only storekeep he'll deal with. He ain't never hurt nobody... yet. Ever'body steers clear o' him, and nobody's never heard him speak... nary a single word."

They had no clock to keep track of the time, but it must have been well past midnight. No one had left the Hawthorne house; there had been no signs of visible activity since the downstairs lamps were put out two hours ago; but the attic was still dimly lit. Spencer and Brady were nearly out of anecdotes, and the supply of firewood had been exhausted for an hour or more, but the prevailing bed of glowing embers created just the right atmosphere for the bonds of friendship to strengthen. Shawn and Steve had made the perfect contact with the time.

Then, through the stillness of the night, the shrill screech of a squeaky door hinge summoned up goose bumps in wholesale proportions on the four boys closely huddled around the dying fire. Their eyes trained on the darkness behind the mansion, where a single lantern revealed two shadowy figures stirring about near the carriage barn. Spencer immediately recognized the nature of the activity: a horse was being harnessed and hitched to a carriage, the carriage that his father had recently repaired, and the equine was the unmistakable 'Cleo,' an off-white Lipizzaner that the Hawthornes acquired from *the* P. T. Barnum. Cleo was high-spirited but well-mannered, strong but gentle. He was a beautiful beast, but he just didn't measure up to the expectations of a good circus performer. But he handled the gold-pinstriped, cobalt blue phaeton flawlessly as he proudly trotted down the lane from the carriage barn and turned northward into town with the two passengers safely in tow.

"Now where d'ya s'pose them two ol' biddies would be a goin' this time o' night?" And with that question posed but not answered, Spencer and Brady expressed their sincere hopes to meet their new acquaintances again. They bid their farewell and trekked off into the night back to Miller's Pond.

Shawn and Steve settled into the tent and listened for the return of the moonlight riders, as the frogs serenaded them to sleep.

TWELVE

They might have been content with their findings so far, but now Shawn and Steve were drawn into a whole new spectacle of marvel. Spencer and Brady had fueled their desire to discover, and the new esprit de corps could not just be relinquished. A certain social intimacy was established: Spencer and Brady were the direct connection to a society totally obscure from casual visits by the Twentieth Century, and even Shawn and Steve were unsure of the longevity of *their* access, or if it even existed at all, once they returned to 1965.

With the new day, new inspirations were born, too. The town could now be looked upon with a different perspective. It was almost as if they knew some of the people, from the vivid exposé furnished by Spencer and

Brady the night before. Now, many of the faces had names, as well as personalities, and it was easier to understand the dynamics of the lifestyle practiced here. All the books in the Public Library could not have created the realism Shawn and Steve had the opportunity to experience first hand.

Floyd Donovan was behind the counter with his back to the door as they entered the General Store. "Mornin.' How are you boys today?"

Maybe he really did have eyes in the back of his head. Or maybe he had just simply observed Shawn and Steve through the front window as they approached the entrance.

The interior of the store was poorly lit by 1965 standards. The only light was coming in through the windows on either side of the entrance, and two more on the adjacent wall. The wood-planked floor squeaked as it was walked upon, and the air was saturated with a variety of aromas, ranging from vinegar to freshly ground coffee. Two elderly women browsed near the back wall, and a six-year-old was being coaxed by her older brother to decide on the peppermint sticks or the gum drops. The row of penny candy jars were presenting a tough decision for the tike.

Shawn felt compassion for the children as he knelt beside the little boy. "Here... get some of each" he said as he dropped several pennies into the youngster's cupped hand. The few cents from his plentiful stash was of little consequence, but the cheerful smiles on their little faces were worth a million dollars.

Baskets filled with fresh fruits and vegetables lined the floor of the center isle. Beyond them were several wooden barrels displaying painted labels of Vinegar, Molasses, and *Monongahela Whiskey*. More kegs were labeled Crackers and Pickles. A pyramid of fifty-pound, cloth sacks of flour leaned into the corner, and on shelves along the outside wall were bottles of *Heinz Ketchup*, tins of *Log Cabin Syrup*, and cans of *Chase and Sandborn Coffee*. There were boxes and bags of salt, spices and sugar. Raisins, *Saratoga Chips* and pretzels. Peanuts and walnuts still in the shells, baking powder, and *Van Camp's* canned beans. Plenty of the names and commodities were familiar, but this was far from any supermarket atmosphere.

Steve had just located the boxes of matches when Floyd greeted the two women standing in front of the counter with a small basket filled with their desired items. "Good morning Lizzy... Emma." He was one of the few people who *remembered* which of the twins had the mole on her chin.

Shawn and Steve froze as they listened to the conversation at the counter.

"Tomorrow is our birthday. All the boarders are away for a few days, and we're having guests for tea."

Floyd proudly announced to his patrons that he had just yesterday received some Oriental tea all the way from the *A and P* in Milwaukee, but he hadn't picked it up from the railroad station yet. "But if you stop back this afternoon, it'll be here."

The women agreed they *must return* for a sampling of the special tea, and as they turned to walk away, they nearly collided with Shawn and Steve, who had moved toward the counter to get a closer look. And now they were closer than they really wanted to be, staring into the dark, spine tingling eyes of the less-than-attractive old hags, identical twins except for Lizzy's chin mole. Emma and Lizzy Hawthorne glared at Steve, and then Shawn, as if with the surprise of recognition.

Their jutting, square chins and crooked, pointed noses reminded Steve of Elmira Gulch. Had they worn pointed hats and long, black capes, they could have easily passed for the *Wicked Witch of the West*, times two. It certainly wasn't difficult to understand why they had become unpopular as ladies of ill fame.

Without speaking a word, all four gathered their composure. Shawn and Steve stepped aside, as Emma and Lizzy hastily disappeared out the front door.

"How much for this box of matches?" Steve asked.

"Ten cents" Floyd replied without hesitation.

As Steve flipped a dime onto the counter, Shawn was taking notice of the July, 1890 calendar tacked on the wall. A black X marked off each day, one through fourteen.

"Much obliged," Steve said. "We'll probably be back for more supplies later."

At least, now they knew it was Tuesday, the fifteenth of July, but they still had no means of telling the exact time. So like a couple of sailors just after pay day, they dodged the horses and wagons on Main Street and headed for Johnson's Emporium.

A Nineteenth Century version of a department store, this one was much brighter inside than the General Store as it had many large windows letting in the sunlight, and boasted a quite cheery environment for the impressive array of goods it displayed. There was everything from *Justin's* Boots to *Winchester* rifles and *Colt* pistols; *Stetson* hats to pots and pans; currycombs and saddles to orange covered dime novels with titles like *Black Beauty*, *Little Lord Fauntleroy*, and *Adventures of Huckleberry Finn*.

For one of his ten-dollar gold pieces, Steve proudly tied the leather lanyard connecting the shiny, silver-cased pocket watch to his belt loop, and slipped the new watch into his pocket. One more event could be added to the list of reasons this was a special day. This was Steve's first watch. Ever.

They didn't need the watch to know it was getting close to lunch time. Although their lives had been shifted seventy-five years, their stomachs were still on schedule. And today, at the Hotel, they would learn that a beef dodger was a corn meal cake filled with minced beef. Not quite as tasty as the chicken stew, but the apple dumpling for desert was scrumptious.

The train was on schedule, too, making its regular stop

on the two day round trip between cities along the Black River and Milwaukee. Nothing seemed out of the ordinary. The steam whistle still frightened the horses, and a crowd still gathered along the tracks, and the usual freight loading and unloading wasn't much different today than yesterday. For Shawn and Steve, the novelty of the steam locomotive had nearly worn off, and there was little here to hold their attention. Instead, their interest was drawn toward the north end of town, where frequent puffs of smoke rolled into the air. Garett's Blacksmith Shop was in that direction and that seemed a likely spot to begin the rest of the day's exploration.

THIRTEEN

Each time Adam Garett pumped the long bellows handles, the hearth fire intensified and the bed of glowing red coals brightened. Frequently, he pulled the horse shoe out of the coals for inspection, and finally he determined it was malleable enough for the near by anvil and a dozen, or so, shaping blows, followed by a few exacting, gentle taps with the clumsy-looking, heavy hammer. Then, a column of steam rose from the sizzling water bucket as the glowing iron was dipped in, and almost instantly quenched to a cold gray. Adam appeared to know he had an audience, but that didn't slow his pace to check the fit of the new shoe on the huge draft's hoof.

"Gypsy!" Of all the horses in Westland, Steve could identify at least two of them: Cleo, the Hawthorne's white Lipizzaner, and Gypsy, the leader of the Kelly Lumber transport team. Shawn was less impressed with Steve's ability to recognize a horse, and wandered out to where Spencer was splitting firewood. But Steve remained for a few minutes, intrigued by the degree of precision the smithy was demonstrating with the use of only crude tools. Equally amazing was the fact that this very location, in his own time period, was still rendering maintenance for Kelly Lumber vehicles.

Spencer was elated to see his new friends again, but seemed a little disappointed that he would have to spend the rest of the day splitting wood for his father's hearth, and wouldn't have time to socialize.

"That's okay," Steve said eagerly. "You have another ax?" He had split firewood many times, and this would be a good, healthy workout.

Shawn toted the uncut logs from the pile and stacked the split wood against the barn wall as Steve and Spencer kept swinging the double-edged axes, and by four o'clock, Adam was impressed and pleased with three times the hearth fuel he had expected.

Hot and sweaty, the three woodcutters sat in the shade of a soft maple as Brady trotted a bareback dapple gray pony into the yard. He, too, was glad to see Shawn and Steve. "Let's all go skinny dippin' down at Raccoon Holler."

Spencer and Brady had their favorite swimming hole, too, and though Shawn and Steve weren't certain where *Raccoon Holler* was, going for a swim on a hot July day was common practice, and was particularly welcome after the wood chopping workout.

"Pa? Can I go swimmin' now?"

Adam couldn't say no after the outstanding performance at the woodpile. "Just be home in time fer supper," he told the boy. "And give them other fellers an invite to supper, too. I'll tell yer Ma to fix a little extry." Generous hospitality was Adam's way of showing his gratitude for the labor-intense job Shawn and Steve had helped to complete, and he was proud to show off his wife's good cooking skills.

Spencer bridled a docile mare named Aster, boosted Steve up on her back, and jumped on behind him. Shawn joined Brady on the gray pony, and the four of them rode off into the country to the west.

The swimming hole was a well-hidden wide pool in a stream running through a heavily wooded area that Steve and Shawn only knew as being wide-open farm land, and they had never heard it referred to as *Raccoon Holler*. The name, and the creek, had obviously dissipated over the years, and what a shame. It was sad to think such a great place was forever lost to greedy land development. But it was here now, and they were going to enjoy it while they still could.

With horses tied to a tree branch, and clothes heaped on the creek bank, the four frolicked in the cool, refreshing water for the better part of an hour, and nearly another hour just sitting on the creek's edge basking in the solitude and allowing the sun and the breeze to dry them off.

Betty Crocker couldn't have served up a finer feast than the fare that came from Mrs. Garett's summer kitchen. Chipped beef and mashed potatoes, Johnny cake and baked beans, corn chowder and plenty of apple cider. No one was going to bed hungry at the Garett's house that night. And even after all the effort exerted on the meal preparation, she didn't seem to slow down much. When the lamps were all lit, and Adam was settled into a big, comfortable chair in the sitting room, Mrs. Garett continued with her never ending chores. Tonight there were shirts to mend.

Adam Garett's home was more luxurious than Shawn and Steve expected it would be. A large, two story frame structure had been added to the tiny, original log house, and although simple in design, the finishing touches delivered a sort of elegance. On this hot July night, Shawn and Steve could only imagine the cozy atmosphere a crackling fire in the huge, stone fireplace would create on a frosty winter day. And the furnishings here were of no less quality than they recalled seeing in the old Hawthorne house. It seemed evident that Adam Garett was a *very* successful businessman.

FOURTEEN

D ressed in doeskin, shoulder to toe, and a black felt hat adorning his ebony hair tied back in a pony tail, he stood silently in the late afternoon sun with his arms folded around the multi-colored wool blanket clutched to his chest. Black Wolf was right on time. It was Wednesday, and he was in town with his latest creation to barter for the weekly jug of nerve tonic. He looked harmless, but his reputation of being less than sociable was once again affording him a wide berth on the busy street.

"How much d'ya suppose Floyd gets for a jug of his whiskey?" Shawn's question caught Spencer by surprise. Even in 1890 that was not a commodity commonly purchased by a teen-ager.

"I dunno. About a dollar, I reckon."

Shawn had no intention of buying whiskey. His adventurous spirit was headed in another direction. At least a dozen onlookers gasped in fear and held their breath as Shawn approached the old native and held up two silver dollars. Looking into Black Wolf's eyes, he pointed to the blanket, and then to the coins.

As if they were anticipating something horrible to occur, the spectators started backing away. In the past, Black Wolf had always shunned any contact with the white man, except Floyd, with near violent reactions. No one knew why, but there was no reason to question it, either.

And as long as Floyd could successfully broker the goods, many beds would be warmed with Black Wolf's extraordinary blankets.

Shawn's friendly and unafraid expression must have struck harmonious chords. Never witnessed before, a benevolent smile replaced the blank frown on the Indian's seasoned face. He muttered something that sounded to Shawn like "Black Wolf, deal," took the silver dollars, then gently and ceremoniously handed the blanket to its new owner.

Shawn was quite proud of the blanket, and more so the method of acquisition than the blanket itself. No one had ever accomplished such a feat. No one had ever heard him speak. And no one had ever seen Black Wolf crack a smile. *No one.*

Spencer and Brady would be the guests that night as Shawn and Steve reciprocated the hospitality at their campsite. The meal wouldn't be quite so extravagant, nor the beds quite so comfortable. But all that didn't seem to matter. The fraternity was in focus, and somehow, the beans and beef jerky were the perfect entrées for an open air dinner party around a campfire in the woods.

The soiree in progress across the road, though, was a bit more sophisticated. Shawn and Steve were keeping a close watch on the affair, which was creating high levels of curiosity in Spencer and Brady. They didn't understand how a bunch of old women having a tea party could be so interesting, and there was no simple way to explain to them the complexity of the situation. Even Shawn and Steve did not yet realize the circumstances were about to become even more complicated, as well as eye-popping and hair-raising. Before the night was over, they would have a whole new perspective on the house *and* the Hawthorne twins.

Seven smartly dressed women had been welcomed in through the front door, and viewing the goings on with the binoculars, this was apparently the birthday tea party Emma and Lizzy had spoken of at the General Store. They could see the old spinsters moving about, catering to their guests with teapots and pastries, and by the looks of things, there was an ample supply of gossip.

As the evening wore on, the tea guests began departing, until only two remained seated, one at either end of the big oak table. One of the sisters was there, too, and soon the other appeared carrying a fresh pot of tea and refilled the guests' cups. One final toast was made as the four ladies raised their cups, and each took long sips.

Nearly simultaneously, the two visitors seemed to gasp, clutching their throats, and just toppled off their chairs and fell to the floor. The twins sat calmly, and continued sipping their tea as if nothing out of the ordinary had happened.

Astonished, Shawn, Steve, Spencer and Brady watched as all but one of the lamps were extinguished. But they could still see inside as the sisters seemed to be concentrating their efforts near the area where one of their guests had fallen to the floor. It looked as though they were wrapping that woman in a blanket, and then they did the same with the other one. It seemed a little unusual that they had waited so long to come to the aid of the ailing women. And it also seemed odd that the two had fallen in a drunken stupor. That last pot must have contained something stronger than tea.

A dim light appeared from the third story windows about the same time the carriage shed door opened, and Cleo was once again being prepared to power a late-night ride.

Although it sounded risky, Steve convinced his comrades to follow as he circled around to a vantage point where they could better view the rear of the house from the railroad track. Something strange was going on, and his curiosity was now at an all-time high.

Just as he suspected, the two women had not just fallen ill. Nearly concealed in darkness, Lizzy and Emma emerged from the back door of the house struggling with one of the lifeless, blanket-wrapped bodies, and with a certain amount of difficulty, they hoisted it onto the floor of the carriage, then disappeared back into the house. Minutes later, the second body was lying with the first. Emma and Lizzy boarded the buggy and Cleo responded to the "giddy-up" command. Steve could only speculate, but he was quite certain the Hawthornes had poisoned their un-suspecting tea guests, for reasons unknown, and now they were disposing of the bodies.

It was apparent now that Westland had not *always* been the peaceful, crime-free community that Shawn and Steve had always known their entire lifetime. In just a couple of days, they had learned of cattle rustlers, road agents, swindlers, Chicago gangsters, and possibly a trigger-happy Marshall. They had seen evidence of racial discrimination, and the operation of a prostitution house. And now they had witnessed a double murder. Could this really be *their* Westland?

When Cleo and the carriage had vanished into the night, Brady grew a little nervous with the situation. "We better tell Marshall Flagg about this straight away! I told ya them Hawthornes is evil."

"No," Steve said. "Not yet." He wasn't convinced that this was the time to summon the law. After all, the twins *could* be taking those other women to a doctor. Not likely, but possible. He wanted to be sure of all the facts, and if the theory taking shape in his mind was correct, they may not want to inform the authorities at all. "I think I know where they're going, but we'll never keep up with them on foot."

It kind of felt like sneaking Dad's car without permission as they bridled a couple of horses at the Garett stable. But horses don't have odometers or gas gauges, and Spencer and Brady *were* skilled bare-back riders.

"How do you know where they're going?" Shawn was curious of Steve's perception, but Steve didn't want to say anything that Spencer and Brady would hear.

"I'll explain later." There wasn't time, right now, to step aside for a private conversation. By now, the Hawthornes had too much of a head start, and Steve wanted to prove his speculation. They mounted the steeds and Steve told Spencer to lead the way to the Kelly saw mill.

Jasper Valley was as serene as it had ever been. Moonlight reflected from the twisting ribbon of water that gurgled along the bottom land, and the still air smelled of fresh sawdust. But tonight it seemed to hold the eeriness of *Sleepy Hollow*. Never before had Shawn or Steve experienced this kind of apprehension in the place that was always their sanctuary, a natural resort where they could always escape the chaos of everyday frustrations.

Shawn still wasn't sure what Steve was deliberating as they arrived at the edge of the forest overlooking the mill. But when Steve instructed Spencer and Brady to stay with the horses, as he and Shawn would go the rest of the way on foot, Shawn knew it must have something to do with the tunnel. Now he understood why Steve was keeping the information from the others.

There was no mistaking Cleo. The ghostly white form stood out as the lunar glow bathed the landscape. But no one else, dead or alive, was in the carriage. It stood empty by the creek bank.

Only one narrow opening between the huge boulders would allow access to the tunnel entrance without climbing over. If they took the climbing route, they didn't risk the chance of meeting the Hawthornes on their way out. From atop the rocks, looking down toward the passage entrance, they could make out the shape of a human body wrapped in a blanket, motionless. Still determined to be sure of all the facts, Steve jumped down to confirm the object's identification. It was definitely a human body.

As he rejoined Shawn, Steve began to explain his theory of this bizarre scenario. The tales they had been told about the Hawthorne sisters now seemed to be more fact than legend. They had faked their own deaths by placing the two bodies of women similar in appearance to themselves in the house, to be found later, somewhat decomposed. In 1947 there wouldn't have been the forensic technology to make positive identification. It would have just been assumed the bodies found in *that* house were those of Lizzy and Emma Hawthorne.

Shawn had some skepticism. "The *Hawthorne* bodies were found and buried twenty years ago. Why are we witnessing the act now?"

Steve continued with his theorizing. "We couldn't control the time we arrived here, but maybe the Hawthornes know how to do that. They have come here from a different time. We came from 1965. They came from 1947."

Though this entire ordeal seemed rather staggering in terms of reality, Steve's theory was as valid as the fact that they *were* in 1890 Westland, and now, *almost anything* seemed possible. Now it didn't seem so impossible for the Hawthorne twins to appear in that house ten years after their alleged deaths. *They weren't dead!*

There wasn't any point, now, to try to stop what was already done. Emma and Lizzy would soon return for the second body and right or wrong, the boys had to let history take its unaltered course.

FIFTEEN

Cleo stood like a stone sculpture in the early morning sun, and there was no sign of any other activity in or near the mansion. Steve sat alone watching the sunrise as the others slept, all snuggled under Shawn's newly acquired Indian blanket. With a lot on his mind, he figured he would have some time to himself, and this would be a good time for meditation.

The Hawthornes had committed a near perfect crime. The cadavers would never be found in this time, and when they *would* be discovered, there would be no reason to suspect they weren't those of Lizzy and Emma Hawthorne, as no one else of that era would be missing. The two women were victims of more than the brutal act of murder. The post-mortem mistaken identity would deny them the dignity of proper burial rituals, and their disappearance would remain a mystery for all eternity.

There was not much Shawn and Steve could do or say without exposing themselves, or revealing the secret of the tunnel. And maybe nothing *should* be done, considering the impact of altering history. But what and how much could Spencer and Brady be told? Although a close, trusting relationship was established, this was a delicate situation, and somehow, they would have to be kept silent, too. Steve knew he and Shawn had captured the loyalty and admiration of their new friends, so it shouldn't be too difficult to convince them to pledge their allegiance to secrecy.

Steve's concern and the desire to discover the *true* story behind the Hawthorne legends was building. There were so many unknown facts, and simply speculating was not satisfying his curiosity. The answers were attainable, and he was determined to uncover them.

"The Hawthorne sisters seemed to recognize us at the General Store yesterday," Steve thought over and over. It didn't seem likely that they had ever met before, or that Lizzy and Emma had ever seen them prior to the store meeting... or had they? He and Shawn had been in close proximity to their house on many occasions, and just because they had never sighted the twins, that didn't mean the twins couldn't have observed them watching the house from the rose garden gazebo during the many late night electrical storms.

And if the Hawthornes really were using the corpses of the other two women to fake their own deaths, why were they taking such drastic measures to make everyone in 1947 believe they were dead? Were they running from something, or someone? Why didn't they just disappear? They certainly had access to the best and most secure escape route anywhere on the planet.

Steve was glad to see Shawn stirring before the others awoke. They had a lot to discuss privately, and they needed Spencer and Brady to swear to an oath of secrecy. Steve had a plan for that. He already had a ritual contrived that would be administered, and literally carved in stone, once they moved their campsite to the rocks, which was first on Steve's list of priorities. This campsite was beginning to feel a bit uncomfortable and maybe even less safe now. The rocks would provide more security. If the twins *did* recognize them, and considering the circumstances that developed over night, this camp was just too close.

Trying to be as ceremonious as he could be, Steve made up the oath of secrecy as he went along, and it seemed to be holding Spencer and Brady in a vigilant state, as he used his hatchet to chisel a large X on the back side of one of the huge boulders, then carefully formed all their initials, one in each section of the X. When he was finished, Spencer and Brady watched with fright in their eyes as Steve held the hatchet toward the sky, and petitioned in a pleading voice to the God, *Mr. Firestone*, to protect them all against the evils they had witnessed, and to help them keep their lips silent in order to preserve their safety.

Now that it was established that no one would say a word to any living soul about the previous night's incident, Spencer and Brady had to go home to perform their daily chores, but they would return again later that evening.

"Do you think they bought it?" Steve was still a little concerned.

"Oh, they bought it, all right," Shawn replied. "And *you*! You ought to have your own travelin' medicine show."

There wasn't time for exploration that day. Hours would be spent just discussing what had transpired, and what the next steps to discovery should be. And there was so much to consider.

The Hawthornes had chosen that particular night to commit the deed—their birthday—and that seemed consistent with the stories Shawn and Steve had always heard. That was the main basis for Steve coming to the conclusion they were faking their deaths in 1947. But why were they doing it? Many possibilities existed, but Steve couldn't help thinking it was because they were either wanted by the law, or the lawless. Something, or someone was causing them to create a diversion, and a couple of dead, unidentifiable bodies would do just that. If the legends were anywhere near accurate, and with the distinction the Hawthornes and their house had gained over the years, it was unlikely that anyone would go searching through that house, until two adventurous young boys, in 1965, would be overcome by their inquisitiveness and break in through a cellar entry just to take a look. But the twins hadn't counted on that happening. They had created a ghoulish reputation surrounding the house by allowing themselves to be seen for a while after they were *dead*, and that should have kept everyone away for all time. Then, by covering the third story windows, they could stay, and move about without being detected in a sanctuary protected by ghostly lore. And because they could not enter or exit by the normal usage of the doors, the tunnel was their only means of coming and going. The construction of the dam and the lake in Jasper Valley in 1957 ended it all.

Shawn and Steve had formulated a workable, conceivable account, considering the first-hand information they had recently accumulated. But the one question of *why* hadn't been answered yet.

"There's only one way we're ever going to learn the rest of the story." Steve was determined to find the answers, and he knew what they had to do.

"And what way is that?" Shawn was curious, too, but Steve had been three steps ahead of him since yesterday, and so far, Steve's theories seemed quite logical, so there was no reason not to follow his lead.

"We have to go to 1947... through the tunnel."

"But we don't know how to control the time we arrive at the other end."

"We didn't when we came here, but we do now. Last night, when we saw the twins come after the second body, I noticed they weren't in the green light very long... not as long as we were... so I counted the seconds they were in it when they went back. Four seconds. Only four seconds. That must put them into this time in 1947. There's no reason it can't work for us, too."

That fourth dimensional jump would put them into Westland just one year before they were born, so it was a safe bet they wouldn't meet themselves, if their timing was right. But plenty other people they knew *would* be there, including their parents. Of course, not even their mothers and fathers would recognize them. How could they? They weren't born yet. The only ones who would recognize Shawn and Steve in 1947 were the Hawthorne twins, and they would probably be making themselves scarce, until long after the corpses were discovered.

Emergence from the cellar trap door would be the only risky part of the trip, but if they were careful, no one would detect them exiting the house in the middle of the night. And when they had gained the knowledge they were after, they would simply return to the valley, come through the tunnel light as they had done the very first time, and return home to 1965.

It was a simple plan, and it didn't appear to be any more hazardous than anything they had already experienced.

The sun was dipping below the tree tops when Spencer came running across the clearing behind the rocks. Something was wrong. His expression was one of distress. "Ya can't stay here. Marshall Flagg's gettin' up a posse and they're huntin' fer you!"

"What do ya mean, huntin' us?"

"I heard my Pa and him talkin' today. He even asked me when I last saw ya."

"But *why* is he lookin' for us?"

Spencer caught his breath, and then explained what was happening.

While Shawn and Steve were theorizing, studying, and

planning all day, the whole town was buzzing with gossip. Marshall Flagg had turned the crank on the rumor mill when he began asking questions of the citizenry regarding the report of the missing Alice Page and Wilma Kerns. They had not been seen since last night at the Hawthornes' birthday party, and when Flagg's investigation lead to the Hawthorne home, Emma and Lizzy assured him that all their tea guests had left, Alice and Wilma being the last. That's when Lizzy insisted that the two young strangers who were hanging around town must be the ones responsible for the disappearance.

Suddenly, Shawn and Steve were fugitives, and until a method to amend the inequitable allegation was invented, the best plan was to hide. Spencer was convinced the loft in his father's barn would be the safest place, as the Marshall had already looked there. They could hide out there until it was safe to make their get-away once the Marshall believed they had left the territory. Spencer and Brady would sneak food to them, and ensure their temporary refuge would provide the necessary protection.

Two days and nights of camping in the hayloft, unable to get out into the fresh air, not only produced plenty of time to calculate and plan. It also made two very anxious spirits, and by late Saturday afternoon, Shawn and Steve were ready to take their chances on making a run for it.

The Marshall's posse had been unsuccessful in sniffing out victims or suspects. There was not a trace of Alice Page or Wilma Kerns. Never before had a disappearance been so absolute. And now the trail of the only suspects was cold, too, and it appeared as though the intensity of the search was greatly reduced.

Spencer and Brady came to the loft that night with the good news, but with heavy hearts, as well. They knew Shawn and Steve would disappear into the night, never to return. This was going to be a painful parting. The four had shared a brotherhood born of the same doctrine that kept Shawn and Steve always on the same page. Though the companionship was being cut short, the friendships would last forever, and the memories of the past week would live on in each of them for all time.

There wasn't an easy way to just end this brief but special time they had spent together. Steve sensed the sadness gripping Spencer. "Hang on to this, for good luck and to remind you of our friendship." It might have only seemed like a token to Steve, but to Spencer Garett, the five-dollar gold piece Steve put in his hand was the grandest, most meaningful present he had ever received. Although five dollars was a lot of money, Spencer recognized the coin *not* as a financial windfall, but as the symbolism for which it was intended.

A tear might have trickled down Brady's cheek, but he wiped it away before the others would notice, as Shawn presented him with a Half Eagle, as well, and offered the same "good luck" sentiments. It was a gift Brady Pendleton would treasure always. He, too, saw the memorial of a remarkable fraternity—one that could never be duplicated or equaled.

The horses were bridled and waiting, and now it was dark enough for Spencer and Brady to ride their passing friends safely out of town without being noticed. Knowing they would never see this sight again, as the bare-backed steeds trotted them quietly toward the valley Shawn and Steve glanced over their shoulders to the darkened Westland downtown, and to the silhouette of the church steeple standing tall above the treetops in the moonlight. If their calculations were right, the next time they saw that steeple, more than a half century would have passed, and that steeple would be one of the only remaining sights here now. Spencer and Brady would be old men, hardly the allies they could count on in 1947. That is, unless they were told the secret Shawn and Steve had protected so well all this time.

They had nearly reached the Kelly saw mill where Steve requested to be the point of departure, a destination that had Spencer quite curious. As Shawn and Steve dismounted with their bags of gear, Steve was just about to confidentially confer with Shawn on the subject of arranging a meeting with Spencer and Brady in 1947. But the silence of the night was interrupted by a thunderous pounding of horses' hooves—*many* horses.

Spencer knew there wasn't time for any lengthy good-byes. "Somebody must've seen us leavin' town, and they're followin' us. Get outa sight in the woods. Me and Brady will ride up the valley and lead 'em off in the other direction so you can get away. Good-bye Steve. Good-bye Shawn, and good luck."

With those words, Spencer Garett and Brady Pendleton vanished into the shadowy hills beyond the saw mill, and Shawn and Steve were barely ducked into the brush at the edge of the dense forest when eight horsemen galloped by just a few feet from where they were crouched out of sight. Hardly visible in the dim moonlight across the valley, Spencer and Brady appeared, and when they knew they had been spotted by the posse, they rode off again with the eight determined horsemen in hot pursuit.

Somehow, Shawn and Steve knew that Spencer and Brady would be okay, and now, thanks to their brave comrades, they had time for a much needed bath in the creek before they started their journey into the next century.

SIXTEEN

"One thousand-one... one thousand-two... one thousand-three... one thousand-four."

Transversing the tunnel, this time, with only the illumination of one candle that wouldn't stay lit if they walked too fast, was more time consuming and tedious than the previous trips had been. The slippery, stone stairway leading to the Hawthorne cellar was a welcome sight, although they weren't totally certain what awaited them at the top.

As they swung open the heavy wooden door, the stench was nearly overpowering. They had experienced the foul odors of pig sty, dead animals, and garbage dumps, but the magnitude of this far exceeded anything they knew. There was little doubt that the bodies of Wilma Kerns and Alice Page were in that house, and the July heat was performing the intended function. Shawn and Steve were thankful, at that moment, that they were familiar with the location of the exit, and they wasted no time in getting to it. No matter how intense their curiosity, there was to be no investigation of the upper levels of the house on this trip.

The outside air was hot and humid, but breathable, and a relief from the torturous environment they had just passed through. As they sat on the ground in the dark back yard, gasping the fresh air, they suddenly realized they had not taken the planned caution when exiting the trap door, and their exposure to *anyone* in this place and at this time would not be favorable. The residence surely would soon be in the scrutiny of the authorities, and they didn't want to give anyone a reason to connect them to the event that was already in motion.

As planned, the railroad tracks offered the most subtle route away from the scene. Two blocks from here, a side street led to the eastern edge of town where they could take refuge in the woods at the top of the ski hill. That was the nearest place they were sure of being unchanged that would provide some security, and until they had a chance to scope the town in the daylight, and get a better feel of the *new* surroundings, it was probably safer to stay out of sight.

Dawn delivered a dreary, dismal day over Westland. But despite the lack of sunshine, the heat and humidity was unmerciful without even a whisper of a breeze.

It seemed a little unusual at first that this still wasn't the city they expected to see. There were definitely signs of development and progress and growth, but not to the degree they had anticipated. This *was* still a few years before their earliest recollections, and maybe they were just expecting too much.

Several houses flanked the now paved Main Street, and nearly all of the box elders and sumac were gone. The beginnings of a park contained newly planted maples, one small flower bed surrounding a flag pole, and a half-dozen wooden benches.

And just across the street from the park, right where it was supposed to be was the Hawthorne house, less attractive now than the last time they saw it. The paint was peeling and the yard was full of weeds. It was definitely showing signs of neglect.

Very little traffic was moving on the streets—just a few pick ups and small delivery trucks. Westland had grown in size, but it seemed to have regressed in liveliness. It wasn't the usual bee hive of activity. Steve took notice of the vehicle vintage. All the cars and trucks were much older than he thought he would be seeing. Shawn justified that by reminding him that this was just after World War II, and maybe newer cars were still hard to get.

But then Shawn noticed something that didn't quite ring true to him. Kelly Lumber Company was a much lesser version than it should be. The meek little building was in the right location now, but he had always been told that his grandfather expanded the retail business on Main Street considerably by the mid-1940s, and this certainly didn't have the characteristics of considerable expansion.

But this *had to be 1947*. The dead bodies were in the house. The horrible stench in there couldn't be anything else. All the stories of the Hawthorne twins ended with the certainty of their deaths occurring in 1947. So if this was to be their staged final exit, this *had to be 1947*.

They sat there on the park bench for a couple of hours,

confused, and maybe a little worried about how they might already be responsible for changing the course of history. Could they have unknowingly tampered with the natural order of mankind? Could they have created a forward motion deficiency and sent Westland into being a backward community of poverty? What was life to be like when they returned to 1965? *IF* they could return to 1965. Guilt was slowly taking command of their feelings, and they were nearly convinced they had plunged their town into doom, without knowing how or why. There had to be a way to put time and legend into proper perspective.

"What ya lookin' at?"

Their near hypnotic condition allowed a young man to approach unnoticed. The silence that had prevailed for at least fifteen minutes while they merely stared across the street at the old house was broken by a voice neither Shawn nor Steve recognized.

"Ah… we were just passin' through… happened to notice that house across the street."

"That's Lizz and Emma Hawthorne's house… quite a place, isn't it? Used to be a lot nicer-lookin' but lately they kinda let it go to hell."

"My name is Steve."

"And I'm Shawn."

"Pleased to meet you, Steve and Shawn. I'm Jesse."

Once again, Shawn and Steve sensed an immediate friendship generating, and right now, the one asset they needed more than anything was a trusted friend in this stranger-than-expected environment.

Steve was interested in learning how deep Jesse's roots grew in Westland. "You lived here all your life?"

"All twenty years of it." Jesse ruffled his already uncombed, short blonde hair, wiped the sweat from his forehead with his sleeve, and unbuttoned his faded denim shirt in an attempt to get a little relief from the heat.

"I live with my grandparents now. My mother died when I was three, and my father was killed in a logging accident about ten years ago, but Mr. Kelly has always made sure I was taken care of. Pop worked for him when he was killed."

In defiance of the infernal heat, a chill went down Shawn's back. Once again, he was glad he had not mentioned a last name, and now it was certain he couldn't. Jesse must have been referring to his grandfather, and although he felt relieved to hear a heart-warming report of his ancestry, he didn't want to hear any more.

"So...what do you do here in Westland?" That seemed the most logical question to ask to get the conversation moving in a different direction.

"Well... these days there isn't a whole lot to do here. Lots of people lost everything they had last year when the stock market crashed...some businesses just locked the doors. And I heard that even the bank is in trouble now, so there aren't many jobs to be had. I'm lucky enough to get some work at the depot on the days the train comes through twice a week loading and unloading baggage and freight. Last month, three brand- spankin'-new Model A's came in, and I got to drive them down the ramp off the flat car. Someday I'm gonna buy a Model A. Then I can travel around the country and find me a *good* job."

Despite his star-crossed childhood, and the seemingly distraught environment he was living in, Jesse still displayed a permanent, natural smile and there was a sparkle in his blue eyes. The plaguing rough times he had just described didn't seem to dampen his spirits, and never before had Shawn or Steve encountered a person with such enthusiastic optimism. Although Spencer Garett and Brady Pendleton were impressively strong in that category, they couldn't compare to Jesse's exceptional attitude and greater intellect.

"So...what d'ya do when you're not working?"

"Grandma and Grandpa have a lot of books, and I read quite a bit."

That was Shawn's foot in the door. "I'll bet there's a whole library in that house over there."

"Yeah... there is. But how did you know that?"

"Oh... just a hunch. What else do you know about that house?"

Jesse's face revealed a devilish grin as he considered the possibility that Shawn and Steve might be a pair of nomadic desperadoes shrewdly in search of their next target. It wouldn't affect his friendship with them, but it *would* warrant a suggested realignment of their judgment. "If you're planning on breaking into *that* house, I'd reconsider if I were you."

"No way. We wouldn't *think* of doing something like that." Shawn knew that statement was teetering on the threshold of a lie, but he hoped he had been convincing enough to keep Jesse from formulating some adverse opinions regarding their presence in Westland. But now, Jesse had stirred his curiosity even more. He seemed to know more about the Hawthornes and their house, and somehow, Shawn was going to get him to tell the story.

"Have you ever been inside it?"

Jesse didn't appear too shaken by their inquisitiveness, or reluctant to provide the answer, and then some.

"Yeah, I've been inside a few times. Lizz and Emma Hawthorne take a lot of trips to Milwaukee on the train, and when they get home, they pay me fifty cents to haul their baggage back to their house. They always invite me in for a cup of tea when I get there. And when Mr. Capone comes to visit, he pays me five bucks to wash his car in the back yard. He's a millionaire, you know."

Their eyes widened as Shawn and Steve huddled closer, and to be sure they correctly understood Jesse's delivery, they exclaimed in unison, "Capone?"

"Yeah... Capone... *Al Capone*... you must've heard of him. *Everybody's* heard of Al Capone."

Shawn and Steve just nodded in acknowledgment with their ears perked to Jesse's every word.

"Mr. Capone and his boys have been visiting the

Hawthornes quite regularly," Jesse went on. "I think they stop off on their way to his place up north. They'll get here in the evening, spend the night, then take off again the next day, heading north. They've been doing this for a couple of years now. Lizz and Emma must have something real special going on with Capone. He's always bringing stuff to them. Last spring, a truck pulled up to the door and they unloaded a fancy billiard table. Now, every time Capone and his men come to stay over night you can see them shootin' pool, there, in the upstairs windows.

"But lately, it seems that Capone's visits haven't been so friendly. Something must've happened between them. I think it must have something to do with the girls he brought here to stay with the Hawthornes. They just disappeared. Rumor is that they were prostitutes Capone brought in from out East, New York or Philadelphia. It's kinda strange, too. They were here for a while, and then one day they were just gone, and no one saw them leave, and no one's seen them since. Pretty young things, they were, too.

"Lizz and Emma got on the train for Milwaukee last week. They're usually gone for a week at a time, so I reckon they'll be on the next train day after tomorrow. When I take their bags to the house this time, I'm gonna ask them how much they'd pay me to trim the weeds in their yard, and maybe even repaint the house. It sure could use a coat of paint… and I could sure use the money."

A few sprinkles of rain plummeted from the gloomy

sky. There was no doubt a good soaker was needed, but Shawn and Steve were not exactly prepared for that kind of weather now. The makeshift canvas tent wasn't going to provide adequate shelter from the approaching storm.

"I'd invite you to our house for the night, but Grandma doesn't like me to bring friends over, but there's an old hay barn no one uses any more outside of town just out past the church. You can take cover there tonight if this storm amounts to anything, and maybe I'll see you again tomorrow."

As Jesse sprinted away across the park, Shawn and Steve gathered up their totes and headed for the town's center, hoping to find the likes of a grocery store. Their food supply was nearly non-existent.

"Do you suppose we should tell Jesse tomorrow that he won't be cutting weeds or painting the house?"

"Nah... but we *should* tell him not to drink any more tea at the Hawthornes'"

Shawn, being a well-read history student, was overflowing with a fountain of recalled information. On the way to the abandoned barn, after acquiring cans of pork and beans, sliced peaches, and a loaf of bread from the sparsely stocked store, he began to spell out the facts of their current predication in time.

"This *can't* be 1947. Considering the condition of everything here, now, Jesse must be talking about the beginning of the Depression when he spoke of "the stock market crash last year." That happened in 1929. So this must be 1930.

"And brand-new Model As? Certainly not a car of 1947. And then there's the part about Al Capone; he was put in Federal prison for tax evasion in 1931, and..."

Shawn paused a few seconds contemplating the validity of Jesse's story. "Do you think he can be talking about *the* Al Capone? *The* Chicago gangster?"

Steve shrugged his shoulders. "Sure... why not? How many Al Capones could there possibly be?"

The vacant barn was just where Jesse said it would be. It was nothing more than a shed with one large open door at one end and no windows. A layer of loose, dry hay covered the floor. Not exactly the Hilton, but at least it was a roof over their heads. Now that the rain was beginning to fall more heavily, that old barn suddenly *was* the Hilton.

Now that they determined what year they had stumbled into—1930 and *not* 1947—Steve's theory for the purpose of the bodies lying in the Hawthorne house didn't seem to fit into the scheme of things. If the twins were attempting to mock their own deaths, and they allowed the public to see them leaving town on the train, they hadn't done a very good job of covering their tracks. And this was just 1930. It was a well-known fact the Hawthornes would remain in Westland another seventeen years. Surely, this was not the final departure meant to be the flimflam that would remove them from the census. The corpses were bound to be discovered soon, and the Hawthorne sisters would be exonerated of any wrong-doing. History mandated their escape from prosecution, and insured their undeserved freedom.

Though it seemed to be a collision course with an impenetrable brick wall, there had to be more pieces of the puzzle yet to be considered. As they drifted off to sleep to the sonata of the rain on the tin roof, the rumbling thunder, and the whistling wind, they were thankful that, at least, 1930 had allowed them an escape from the rigorous pursuit of Marshall Flagg's posse.

SEVENTEEN

He heard the sparrows chirping, and a dog barking somewhere off in the distance long before Steve opened his eyes to yet another gray, overcast day. The rain had stopped sometime during the night, and now the only visible indication of the passing storm was a puddle of water just outside the barn door, rippled by a gentle breeze. Occasionally, a flock of sparrows would gather around the tiny pond like tourists on a beach. They seemed so pleasantly fascinated with the newly created neighborhood pool.

Shawn awoke as Steve handily removed the lids from the canned peaches with his hunting knife. He handed one of the cans to Shawn. "Here. I made breakfast."

They had sufficed with much less on a number of previous camping excursions, so all things considered, these accommodations weren't all that bad. They had kept dry through a thunderstorm, slept quite comfortably on a soft bed of hay, and now they were dining on sliced cling peaches. They couldn't expect much better than this.

"You know," Shawn said, as he slurped down the last peach slice, "if this *is* the Depression, and with the amount of money we have between us, we would be considered quite wealthy in these times."

Steve contemplated their financial status. "Then I think we should *definitely* have lunch in the finest restaurant we can find."

"Well, I wouldn't count on finding *too* many *fine* restaurants in Westland *in 1930.*"

As it had in the past, and would in the future, the Prairie Lutheran Church steeple towered magnificently above the city. Shawn couldn't help but think, as they hiked past the mighty structure, what a remarkable history that steeple had witnessed over the decades from the days of the pioneers' prairie schooners, to the age of space travel. And although he had only viewed a microscopic portion of it, he was confident that no one else ever had the opportunity to *experience* Westland's vividly graphic chronicle as he and Steve were doing right now.

Just as yesterday, not many people were moving about. Westland now was a ghost town in comparison to the city Shawn and Steve were accustomed. The only consolation was that they understood the circumstances, and it was comforting to know these conditions would all pass in time, and that their home town would some day be restored to the lively metropolis it was always meant to be. For now, they had to ignore the current ambient factors, and concentrate their efforts on why they were here in the first place. The Hawthorne sisters had created a mystery for them to solve, and they were feeling a desperate need to do just that.

The rest of their theory had fallen apart, but one fact was for sure: the billiard table on the second floor that had puzzled them at the very beginning of this adventure was put there and used by Al Capone, a hero to some, but a murderous gangster to most. Lizzy and Emma Hawthorne had a connection, friendly or otherwise, to one of the most notable figures in American history within the society of illicit activity.   That is, if Jesse had his story straight. Shawn and Steve could only assume, at this point, that he did.

It seemed peculiar that the bodies of Alice Page and Wilma Kerns had not yet been discovered, although, during the entire time Shawn and Steve observed the Hawthorne dwelling since their arrival in *this* era, not a single living creature had even come near it. It appeared as though the invisible barrier that protected it from intruders and vandals throughout the '50s and '60s was already in full effect. Jesse confirmed that the ill-natured social attributes of the Hawthorne sisters must have stemmed back long before the days the legends were born, and long before Emma and Lizzy forevermore parted company with Westland's surviving society. His adamant recommendation to evade confrontation with that particular piece of real-estate corroborated every word of warning Shawn and Steve had ever heard.

By mid afternoon, absolutely nothing had happened

across the street, and as the minutes and the hours ticked by, Shawn was beginning to lose his patience. "I say we go over there and look through the windows. Maybe those dead bodies aren't even in there."

Steve wasn't exactly in favor of the peeping Tom plan, and although he didn't think it was a very good one, Shawn did have a point. And in the absence of an active neighborhood, there was little danger of being seen, even in broad daylight. With plenty of experience in stealth approach to that house, they knew the best route was from the railroad, and this time they wouldn't wait for darkness. If they were going to detect anything inside, they would have to make their move before dusk.

EIGHTEEN

They strolled nonchalantly across the yard from the tracks toward the back of the house. The thought of what they would see inside raised goose bumps and made their spines tingle. But now it seemed necessary and they were compelled to learning all the facts, no matter how gruesome the facts were.

Just as Steve was about to peer through the window which he knew would reveal the kitchen, an intrusive distraction cut the attempt short of its goal. The crunching sound of car tires on the gravel driveway, and the purring of an engine pierced through the still afternoon air. Along side the house, the long, black sedan stopped, and as Shawn and Steve peeked around the corner with curious awe, the car doors swung open and four men dressed in dark-colored, pinstriped suits and black hats emerged. One of the men had a white carnation on his lapel. The driver stood guard at the side of the car, as the other three strutted toward the house.

"Wow," Shawn whispered. What kinda car is that?"

"A '29 or '30 Packard, I think." Steve wasn't absolutely certain, but it was a good guess. It surely wasn't a common Ford or Chevy, and these guys weren't door-to-door salesmen.

"Do you suppose that's who I think it is?"

"Shhhh!" Steve heard the vigorous knock on the door and he wanted to hear the conversation between the men that was audible, but not clear enough to understand. There was another rap on the door, and then in a sweet but stern tone, a voice from the porch called out: "Emma? Lizzy? It's me, Al."

There was a quiet pause, and then it sounded as if the door was flung open, and moments later, it slammed shut again. But the men had not entered the house. Their footsteps could be heard on the porch deck, and they were talking but still not loud enough for Steve to make out what they were saying. He heard what sounded like hard-soled shoes clicking down the steps, and then nothing.

It had been totally quiet for a couple of minutes. Steve looked to the black car in the driveway thinking the men must be returning to it. But even the driver who had not accompanied the other three to the door was not at the car now. They had not been paying any attention to him.

It felt like the grip of death that grabbed them from behind, hoisted them up, spun them around, and pinned their backs to the wall all within a split second. It happened so swiftly, they didn't have time to even think about a means of defense or escape. As the two brutes held them there, helplessly suspended with their feet barely touching the ground, the third man—the one with the carnation on his lapel—instructed Karl, the driver, to return to the car, to make sure no one came near it. He stepped up closer to Shawn and Steve. "What are you boys doing here?" he asked, as he struck a match and lit the cigar clenched in his teeth.

Shawn and Steve were so stricken with terror they could not speak, for only inches away, before them stood the one and only Al "Scarface" Capone staring into their eyes. They knew this could very well be the end of their journey. Certainly a villainous character with the unscrupulous reputation he had acquired would think nothing of leaving two more lifeless bodies lying in the back yard of a house in this small town. Was their final thrill in life to be so briefly in the company of this celebrated criminal?

"It's okay, Mr. Capone. They're friends of mine. Don't hurt them. They're okay."

Jesse's rescuing plea came from out of nowhere, and was the sweetest sound Shawn and Steve could have expected. On Capone's signal, the henchmen released their captives, and backed away. Jesse was now poised next to Capone, offering his hand in a friendly gesture of greeting.

"Good to see you, Al. Did you have a nice trip?"

The message to Shawn and Steve in Jesse's eyes was quite clear: *shut up and let me do the talking.* He obviously had a stronger relationship with Capone than he had let on before, as the mobster seemed to immediately recognize Jesse, and there was no doubt he trusted the word of the smiling, blond-haired youngster.

"Hello, Jesse," Capone said. "I wired Lizzy last week. Told her we'd be here today to collect. Things were gettin' a little hot in Chicago, anyway. It was a good time to spend a few days at the cottage up north."

Not only did Capone and Jesse have an established affinity with one another, *they were on a first name basis.* And as long as Jesse maintained a friendly status with them, Shawn and Steve were somewhat confident they would have little to fear of Capone and his boys. They would follow Jesse's lead, and keep quiet.

Jesse began to offer some information. "Lizz and Emma aren't here. They—"

Capone interrupted. "Oh, they're here, all right, but they're laid out on the sitting room floor, dead as a pair of mackerels on a beach. And the inside of the house stinks worse than a morgue run out of ice. Looks like we aren't going to collect today and we won't be doing business here *anymore.*"

Jesse's expression turned to a puzzled frown. It was the first time Shawn and Steve had seen his face without a contented, cheerful smile.

"Does that mean I won't be seeing you any more?" Jesse seemed almost devastated.

"Not unless you come with us right now and work for me. I'm not coming back here. Don't want to get nailed for snuffing out the Hawthornes. This wasn't a very profitable operation, anyhow."

"No," Jesse replied. "Thanks for the offer, but I have to stay here and look after my Grandma and Grandpa. But as soon as I get enough money saved up to buy that Model A, maybe I'll come visit you sometime."

Steve noticed the look of compassion in Capone's eyes.

Shawn was curiously concentrating more on Jesse's oration of intent to continue the association.

Capone leaned toward Jesse, put his hand on Jesse's shoulder, and spoke more quietly, as if to shroud the conversation with a little privacy. "I know you've been saving a long time for that car. How much are you short?"

Without hesitation, Jesse humbly replied with the figure he knew too well. "Three hundred and fifty dollars, but what I make at the depot, it'll be a long time before I have enough."

Al Capone retrieved a bankroll from his pocket and began counting out bills. "Here. Take this. It's enough to get you that Model A, and maybe a little left over."

"But Al... I can't..."

"Take it. It's yours. Just remember... you didn't see me here today, and make *damned sure* your friends understand *they didn't see me, either.*"

Jesse was either a very good actor, or he sincerely *was* moved by the developing situation. Shawn wasn't certain which, as Jesse's bewildered grimace lingered.

"Don't be sad, kid. Mark this day as a new beginning. Now I have to get out of here. And give my regards at the funeral."

Capone and his entourage wasted no time to board the limo. Jesse was right there, and made another attempt to inform Al that the Hawthornes would be returning on the next train, but Karl sped away before he could get it all out. Al Capone was gone for good, and by the look on his face, as he watched the black sedan disappear down the street, so was a part of Jesse. His secretive alliance with a man who not many knew the way Jesse did had abruptly come to a bittersweet conclusion.

Shawn and Steve were still overwhelmed with the association between their newfound friend and the Mafia boss, and the chain of events they had just witnessed. This might have defined why Jesse could sustain such a buoyant disposition during such stressful times. He probably had few worries thinking he was within the protective circles of *the organization*. But he probably *wasn't* aware of the dangers that lurked in Capone's shadow. Capone had plenty of enemies, as well, who would gun him down in an instant, along with any near by associates, if the opportunity arose. But this was neither the time nor the place to tell him that.

"Are you guys okay?" Jesse asked as he walked back toward Shawn and Steve. A forced smile replaced the frown, but concern was still in his eyes.

"All things considered," Steve replied, "we're doin' just fine. But what about those dead bodies in the house?"

Jesse wasn't yet convinced the corpses were really there. He had to see for himself, so he jumped up onto the end of the verandah and stepped cautiously to the door, peeking in through the window. Certain that the Hawthorne sisters could not have returned from Milwaukee, he slowly opened the door, stepped part way in across the threshold, peered around the half-opened door, and quickly stepped back, slamming the door shut abruptly behind him. He covered his nose and mouth with one hand, nearly gagging from the repulsive rank fumes. Shawn and Steve had already experienced the putrid foulness, and they had no desire to subject themselves to it a second time. They already knew the bodies were *not* those of Emma and Lizzy Hawthorne, and there was no point seeing they were really there. Jesse's confirmation of their presence was good enough.

"C'mon, Jesse," Steve urged. "Let's go over to the park and sit down." At the moment the Hawthorne yard didn't seem to be the most favorable spot to contemplate a reasonable course of action, and the park was distant enough to escape the eerie atmosphere suddenly surrounding the residence.

The three of them sat on the park bench, just staring across the street, without speaking at all for several minutes. Jesse was clearly making an attempt to regain his composure. A portion of his world had crumbled and he was mentally searching for a means to heal the wounds he suffered in the destruction. His ties with a long-time friend were severed, and now the Hawthorne twins—one of his sources of income—were dead. Could this day get any worse?

He soon found the resolution within him, and he realized that none of all this really mattered. His pocket was stuffed full of money, the likes of which would have taken many months to earn, providing the railroad kept operating. And the Hawthornes? They were just a couple of old bats who he could survive without. Now, he didn't have to rely on painting their house in order to afford a Model A.

"I'd better find the Constable and tell him about the Hawthornes," Jesse said. "Don't go anywhere. I'll be back in a little while, okay?"

As Jesse started to walk away, Steve was compelled to give him one bit of information. "But that's not the Hawthornes in the house."

Jesse looked over his shoulder as he kept walking on his mission to make the report to the only peace officer in town. "Who *else* could it be?" He, along with Capone, had fallen for the deception. The Hawthornes really had faked their own deaths, but not for the reason Steve had theorized right from the beginning. The twins *would* return, and the question of why they had choreographed this elaborate production was still a mystery.

NINETEEN

Like three pigeons perched on a window sill, Steve, Shawn and Jesse watched from the park bench as a small, curious crowd gathered in front of the house. The Constable's brown '28 Chevrolet coupe, Dr. Butler's '27 Lincoln, and the undertaker's black panel truck, all parked in the driveway, had drawn considerable attention, but the throng of people quickly began to disperse as two men with towels wrapped around their faces carried the first corpse out on a stretcher, and the disgusting odor drifted to where they were gathered. By the time the second cadaver was being loaded into the panel, no one remained. Even Doc Butler had left as there was nothing more he could do.

As the undertaker drove away, Constable Wade Sheppard spotted Jesse, and started walking toward the park. He was half way when Steve quietly commented on the remarkable resemblance the Constable had to "*Paladin.*" Only Shawn made the connection. The popular television western series "*Have Gun-Will Travel*" would not entertain home audiences for nearly another thirty years. Puzzled, Jesse asked "Who's *Paladin?*"

Sheppard approached, and spoke to Jesse. "Well, the Doc declared them dead, all right. Any dern fool could've told me that. But them gals aren't Lizzy and Emma Hawthorne. They must've been some boarders living upstairs. Don't know who they are... or should I say...

were."

Jesse perked up. "Then *they will be on the next train."*

"Yup," Sheppard replied. "If you saw them get on the train last week like you said, they'll be back tomorrow. I can't imagine they'll take too kindly to their roomers dying in their parlor and stinking up the place like that. You better warn them when they arrive. You'll be the first one to see them. Tell them to come see me before they go home from the depot."

Eager to oblige, Jesse responded to the Constable's request. "Yes, sir. I'll tell them."

Sheppard started back across the street to his car, but only a few steps into the journey he stopped, turned back toward the boys, and posed an after-thought question to Jesse. "By the way, you haven't seen that Capone fellow hanging around lately, have you?"

"No sir. Haven't seen him lately."

One of Shawn's curiosities was answered. *Jesse was a good actor.*

After Sheppard was well out of sight, Shawn initiated the quest for more answers that only Jesse could provide.

"Just how well do you know Al Capone?"

That's all it took to get Jesse talking. Now that Capone was gone, there wasn't any reason to keep his past coalition a secret any longer, especially to the fellows he now considered his new pals.

"Al took a likin' to me the very first time we met a couple years ago. He came into town late one night. Lost, I think. He asked me if I knew where Lizz Hawthorne lived. Well, next thing I knew, I was riding in his car giving Karl directions to the house. When we got there, he said to me, "you're all right, kid," and he stuffed a greenback in my shirt pocket. I didn't know who he was then, but I've been invited to the Hawthornes every time he's come to visit ever since. He taught me to shoot pool, and how to win at poker. I could never beat *him*, but never once did he ever take my money. He always gave it back when the game was over.

"Then, last year, just before he went to jail out East, he brought these girls here, and another truck followed him in that time, too. Guess it was supposed to look like the girls were moving in, and I guess they were. But most of the boxes and trunks were full of liquor. I know because I helped tote it all into the cellar. Al paid me real good that night.

"Lizz and Emma have been selling that bootleg on the sly, and I reckon they were taking in quite a haul on the girls, too. And then while Al was in jail, the girls just disappeared. No one saw them leave, and no one's seen them since. Lizz had just come back on the train from Milwaukee. As usual, I hauled her bags to the house, and as usual, she invited me in for some tea, a special blend she'd picked up at the A 'n P in Milwaukee. While I was sitting at the table in the kitchen waiting for the tea to brew, the girls went down into the cellar, and they never came back up as long as I was there. I never saw them again after that.

"There were a lot of people who weren't real happy with the Hawthornes about that time. Most everyone knew what was going on there, but when word got out that it was Al Capone supplying the liquor and the women, no one dared do anything about it. I guess they were all scared of Al, and they just turned their heads the other way when he came to town. Of course, there were those who were regular customers, too, and they probably didn't care *where* the stuff was coming from.

"When Al finally came back, he was pretty upset to find out the girls were gone, and I don't think he's ever forgotten about that. But the liquor and beer kept coming for a long time, on credit I suspect, and he must not have gotten his payments, 'cause he cut them off a month ago. He looked kind of mad today when he thought the twins were dead. S'pose he figured he wouldn't *ever* get his money. That's why he said he wasn't coming back here again."

Shawn saw the sadness in Jesse's eyes reappear as he spoke of Capone's absence. "But Jesse. You know who Al Capone really is, don't you?"

"I know you think he's a *really* bad son-of-a-bitch, and yes, I've heard all the stories about the stuff that's going on in Chicago these days. But Al never did anything bad to me. In fact, he always treated me real good, like a big brother, and I'll miss him."

The sun had gone down since Jesse began the saga,

and now the frosted round globe street lamps dotted Main Street with blotches of soft glow. Shawn and Steve had hardly spoken a word while they soaked up every syllable of the extraordinary testament. This was a piece of Westland's history that was obviously little-known, and rarely, if ever spoken. It was amazing that a famous figure like Capone could have left his distinct imprint on this city, and the pages of time simply wiped it away, leaving not a trace for posterity.

They all bid their good-byes. Jesse had a busy day at the railroad station head of him. Steve and Shawn had a long night of mystery solving awaiting them at the barn where they could discuss the day's events and Jesse's declamation in unconditional privacy.

TWENTY

The cryptographic conundrum scattered and entangled throughout decades of time was finally deciphering itself. The long trail of unnoticed clues was now being noticed, and strangely making sense. Jesse had filled in the blanks, and he made it understandably clear how and why certain events occurred. Now there were fairly substantial facts to start rewriting the Hawthorne legend.

In the seclusion of that little barn, way into the wee hours of the morning, Shawn and Steve reconstructed the time line paralleling the Hawthornes.

"They probably learned the finer points of running a prostitution business from Capone..." Steve began. "They took that know-how back to the 1800s. Their connection with him explains a lot of other things, too. They suckered him out of a bunch of money, which by 1890 standards made them filthy rich. No wonder they could afford that fabulous mansion back then."

Shawn recalled part of Jesse's story. "The girls we saw that night in 1890 were actually the women Capone brought to the Hawthorne house in 1929. Jesse said they disappeared into the cellar and never came back. That's how they vanished without anyone seeing them leave town.

"When Lizzy and Emma had conned Capone out of as much as they were going to get, they planned the fake death ordeal just for *Capone's* deception. They knew he was coming to see them today. He sent them a telegram a week ago. They knew when to put the dead bodies in the house, knowing it would be him to find them. They left town on the train so everyone else here knew they weren't around when the others kicked off, and just like the Constable said, he didn't know who they were, probably just a couple of boarders. Didn't sound like he was even too concerned.

"And you *know* no one will go into that house snooping around. Not the way that place stinks. Bet they planned that, too."

The Hawthornes had acquired a bundle of cash, and now they were rid of Capone *and* clear of the murders they committed. Now that the bodies of Alice Page and Wilma Kerns were used as decoys to ward off Capone in 1930, then perhaps Emma and Lizzy *actually did* show up as the guests of honor at their own funeral in 1947. If that were the case, then it wasn't they who had revisited the mansion ten years later leaving behind the 1957 issues of the newspaper. Someone had, but who?

"The only others who had any knowledge of the tunnel were the girls," Shawn said. "Maybe it was them."

"What do you mean?" Steve asked.

"Maybe it was those girls who returned to the attic. After the twins died, the girls could have gone back there frequently, and easily ventured out into the town without being recognized after so many years."

"Do you think the ghosts everybody saw was them and not the Hawthornes?"

"It's possible. I can't think of any better solution."

The diabolical probabilities were calculated to a reasonably logical conclusion. It didn't really matter how the Hawthorne sisters managed to elude blame for the deaths of the other two women, but the story still didn't seem to be complete. Once again, a visit to 1947 was necessary.

TWENTY-ONE

The northbound train was just pulling out from the station. Only six passengers had disembarked, and now, only two of them remained on the platform next to the depot. Lizzy and Emma Hawthorne, in long, black dresses stood there watching as Jesse rolled their luggage toward them on a steel-wheeled cart. It rumbled across the planks, and came to rest beside them. Shawn and Steve couldn't hear the conversation, but the content of Jesse's speech was evident by the expressions and body language. The twins' reaction of surprise seemed a bit artificial, but Jesse was buying it. And just as he was instructed to do, he pointed them in the direction of the police station. He would keep their bags until they returned, quite certain that this time they would be delivered somewhere other than the house.

When it was safe, Shawn and Steve came out of hiding and approached Jesse as he began to load some wooden crates that had come off the train onto another cart. They were there to say "good-bye," and they knew this was going to be another sad moment. Another friend was being left behind—one they would never see again.

"You guys take care," Jesse said. "If ya ever get back this way again, be sure to look me up. I'll take you for a ride in my Model A. Maybe we can tour the whole country together."

The calculation was pretty simple: Four seconds in the strange green light in the tunnel had shot them forty years into 1930. One second for every ten years. So just under two seconds should bring them forward to 1947. One-point- seven seconds, to be exact. There was no means of measuring time that precisely, but it was worth a try. A stop in that year would perhaps supply an accurate final chapter. It still wasn't absolutely certain that the twins didn't attempt another masquerade party then, too.

It was still broad daylight when they carefully pushed the cellar trap door open just far enough to test the safety of making their exit. Leaving the premises now would definitely present a degree of danger. They surely didn't want to be seen.

The candles were getting short, and the musty, damp cellar wasn't going to provide very comfortable quarters while waiting for the sun to go down. The wooden kegs were still where they had been before, and seemed to be the only dry spot to sit. One candle was snuffed out to preserve some duration, if the need arose. A decision had to be made, and maybe if they sat in silence for a while, they could determine if there was any activity on the floor above them. This was the first time they had been within the confines of the spooky old house during daytime hours, and was certainly the most dangerous, without the cover of darkness to guard them from detection by anyone outside... or inside.

They had no way of knowing their arrival in this era was more than a month after the Hawthorne sisters had been laid to rest in a small, private cemetery plot, only a couple miles from the edge of town.

The silence was broken by the sound of nails being hammered into the exterior walls. Not realizing what was going on, Steve's curiosity got the best of him, and he convinced Shawn, as well, they had to investigate. The noise was definitely coming from outside, so they could possibly gain access to the first floor in the obscurity of the pantry.

Steve climbed the steep stairway with Shawn close on his heels. He pushed the trap door open, and the two of them climbed a couple more steps, exposing their heads and shoulders above the level of the pantry floor. A blood-curdling scream from outside startled them, and they quickly ducked below the floor, and pulled the trap door closed over their heads. Motionless, they listened, as they could now hear the hysterical conversation between the two carpenters, just outside the kitchen window.

"I'm telling you! I saw two people in there. It's got to be the ghosts of the Hawthornes. I *saw* them in there. I *know* it was them!"

His partner climbed the ladder leaning against the wall beside the window, and peered in through the opening remaining from the lack of one board left to be put in place.

"I don't see anything in there now. Hand me that last board. I'll nail it on. Then let's get the hell out of here!"

Shawn and Steve could hear the hasty hammer strokes and the abrupt ladder removal, and the two men scurrying away, mumbling their intent of never returning to finish the rest of the windows on the other sides of the house.

Now deathly quiet, it was a safe bet there would be no one near the house, and from the carpenter's comment about the Hawthorne *ghosts* it was clear the house was void of any occupants. They had missed the funeral, but at least it was safe to come out of the cellar, and perhaps seek the security of an upstairs room for the time being.

Their hunger was the only contributing factor that made Shawn and Steve venture out that night. The big, brass-framed feather bed in the second floor bedroom was quite soothing, considering this was the first actual bed they had laid on since their visit to 1890 when they were overnight guests at Spencer's home. Dusk was falling on Westland as they awoke from a well-deserved nap. They could now safely get out of the house in the evening shadows, and hopefully there would be an open eating establishment to satisfy their need for nourishment. Dino's Cafe was only a couple blocks away, and it was always open at night; at least it was in 1965. And it would be interesting to see if the burgers were as tasty now, or if that was an art that had to be developed over the next eighteen years.

Big Band sounds, Glen Miller style, filled the interior of the diner. The source was an antique-looking juke box with a rainbow of colored lights, and a curved glass top displaying the 78's and the primitive turntable apparatus. Dino's was bustling with activity. It was probably the only place in town open for business at this hour. Trying to be inconspicuous, they took seats at the counter, and ordered their burgers.

Eavesdropping on the various conversations around the room became quite entertaining, but the one being conducted right behind them proved to be the most interesting. One of the four men seated at the table was obviously the carpenter who had misidentified Shawn and Steve as the Hawthorne ghosts earlier in the day. He hadn't changed his drastically inaccurate and highly exaggerated account of what he *thought* he had seen.

"...And there they were, floating up out of the floor. It was them, all right. I saw them with my own eyes. I know I'm not going back there to board up the rest of those windows."

Not to be outdone, one of the other men told his version of a recent experience. "One night last week... that night we had the thunderstorm... I was walking by the house on my way home from the pool hall. I happened to look up just about the time a bolt of lightning lit up everything, and I saw them plain as day in a window up in the third story..."

A third voice from the same table added his opinion. "I knew when they put those two old hags in the ground out on Harper's Hill that they weren't goin to stay there. I just knew the Hawthornes would come back to keep on tormenting the town somehow."

The fourth man had comments, too. "I heard once that a couple of young girls staying at that house disappeared. They never did find them, and then another time, two other women were found dead in there, too."

Shawn and Steve were holding back the chuckles as they finished the burgers. At the moment, the stories seemed pretty hilarious to them, but to the storytellers, this was serious stuff. They were believing what they wanted to believe, whether it was true or not, and no one was about to alter those misconceptions.

As in any small community, gossip spreads quickly, and this story had made the rounds with record-breaking speed. The carpenter's sighting reinforced the previous rumors with solid-as-granite proof. The earth had rejected those vile creatures, and now, their evil, miserable spirits were lurking still, within the walls of that old mansion. And everyone seemed to agree that if no one ventured near it, the twins would remain there, and could cause no harm.

From all the comments they observed most of the next day while just hanging out on Main Street, the people apparently were quite satisfied it *was* Lizzy and Emma Hawthorne buried in the graves on Harper's Hill. No one was sympathetic over the deaths of the Hawthornes. There didn't seem to be any fortifying reasons that justified their unpopularity, just trivial complaints, mostly of their unsociable nature, their unwillingness to keep their lawn groomed, and it was the older sector of citizens who remembered that place as a den of immorality. And now that they were dead, they were the talk of the town. Having an honest-to-goodness haunted house right on their own Main Street must have been the biggest news to hit Westland since the end of World War II, and that house was certainly receiving its lion's share of local publicity.

Shawn and Steve didn't know where Harper's Hill was located. They had never heard of it before, but it couldn't be far away, and asking the right questions of the right people should lead them to it.

It was starting to appear that the entire ghost sighting ordeal really was just a hoax. Shawn and Steve, themselves, were the essence for part of the legend's beginnings, when they were spotted coming up out of the cellar. Not totally impossible, someone could have been observed through the upstairs windows, too, but it probably wasn't the Hawthorne twins. Imagination on the part of the observers was definitely playing a role.

Exaggeration was filling in the blanks.

For the sake of his own satisfaction, if nothing else, Shawn grew more determined to locate the graves on Harper's Hill. Steve thought it less important, but Shawn finally convinced him that they should seek the obscure little cemetery now.

"If we don't find it now, maybe no one in 1965 will know where Harper's Hill is. The stories all say "they were buried in unmarked graves and forgotten," and now we have the opportunity to find out where those graves are. They shouldn't be too hard to spot. They'll still be kind of fresh. It's only been a month."

"Yeah," Steve agreed. "We *did* come here to find out everything we can."

Now it was a matter of talking to some of the people on the street. Someone here was surely able to give them the answer they needed.

A mature looking man was just exiting the Bank a half block away. He was the person they would approach in hopes of attaining a rapid answer. As the man neared, Shawn turned as pale as the ghosts they had been chasing. He shifted his body around as the man passed by, so as not to let the man see his face. Steve suddenly realized who the man was: Shawn's Grandfather.

"I was afraid of this," Shawn moaned. "Grandpa Kelly died when I was seven. I was hoping this wasn't going to happen."

Steve knew, and remembered well, Grandpa Kelly, too.

140

And now that he had almost come face-to-face with him, Steve better understood Shawn's apprehension of such an encounter, and he could feel Shawn's anxiety. They had been successful, so far, to avoid contact like this. They would have to be just a little more cautious from now on.

"Excuse me..." Steve said to another gentleman he was certain of not being any relation. "Could you tell us how to get to Harper's Hill?"

The man looked at Steve with a strange stare, and then at Shawn. "Dyin' would be *one* way."

That answer was frustration enough, without having to ask again. "No. I mean can you tell us where it's located?"

"Ain't nothin' out there but a graveyard. Why the hell would you want to go there?"

Steve realized now that he had chosen the most obnoxious being on the whole planet, and there probably wasn't any reason to continue the conversation.

They walked down the street a ways, and sought a response from yet another. This man and his wife were pleasant and helpful.

"It's out west of town. Just take the gravel road at the end of the street in front of the Bank. At the first crossroads, go left. It's about a mile from there, but you aren't gonna find anything there any more except a graveyard. It used to be the old Harper place, but even the buildings are all gone now. All that's left is the graveyard where they're all buried, the Harpers and Hawthornes.

Lizz and Emma were the last ones left of the whole clan. They were buried out there just a month ago. Shady characters, they were. Bootleggers back in the '20s and '30s..."

"Thank you. Thank you, very much! You've been a big help. We'll be sure to mention you when we write our book."

The gravel road they were told of would take them past the spot where Shawn's father would eventually build his family's home, and the crossroads was just beyond that at Underwood School. That meant that the Hawthornes' graves were not more than a mile as the crow flies from Shawn's house. They had been by that old cemetery hundreds of times, but there was never any reason to pay attention to it.

And in the event the no marker stories *were* correct, it seemed necessary to visit the site *now,* so they would know exactly their location.

A two-mile walk in the country proved to be a gratifying change of scenery. Shawn and Steve had grown somewhat accustomed to the slower, less hectic pace of the former Westland, and now the post-war industrial age was encroaching their city. They had never viewed their modern generation's lifestyle in this way, but now that they had experienced the utter beauty that once surrounded the community, they wondered if all the technology and development and progress was really a fair trade.

They had almost reached Underwood when Shawn remembered a remark Steve made, and quite frequently he was amazed with the lightning-quick replies Steve could produce.

"When we write our book? May I ask *how* you came up with *that?"*

"Well, the other night you said you wanted to write a book, and if they can write a story about a house in Kansas getting relocated *by a tornado* to a place called *Oz,* then someday, we can write an equally unbelievable story about all *this,* too."

He did it again. Steve always had an answer.

TWENTY-TWO

The tiny, thirty-by-thirty cemetery, encircled by a split-rail fence, placed there only to keep farm machinery from knocking down the tombstones, contained the poorly maintained grave sites of a dozen or so Harpers and Hawthornes, all of which dated back to the 1800s. It wasn't surprising, now, that if Emma and Lizzy were the last remaining members of the clan, there was no one left to carry out the placement of the traditional, hand-carved family headstones. Only a small heap of field stones rested at one end of each of the two recently dug graves. Weeds were beginning to take over, and it wouldn't be long until those plots would be lost to nature, and forgotten by man. At least one small detail of the Hawthorne legend was accurate.

But right next to the unmarked Hawthorne graves, were two more headstones that did not bear either of the names of the rest. Ragweed hid part of the inscriptions, so Steve stomped it down to get a better look. Both read: UNKNOWN WOMAN—DIED 1930.

To everyone else, these were unknown souls, but to Shawn and Steve, the two people buried in those graves were no mystery. *They had names.* They were Alice Page and Wilma Kerns.

Shawn and Steve were the last to see them alive. Shawn and Steve witnessed their murders. And now Shawn and Steve were standing over their graves, concurring that it was bad enough the deaths of these two women were the product of greed, but worse yet, they and their families had been deprived the dignity of a proper burial rite.

"At least," Steve said compassionately, "their names should be on the headstones. Let's put them on there."

He had proven his stone carving talents once before with the same hatchet he was still carrying in his tote. Although his style wouldn't necessarily match that of the other markers there, that didn't seem to matter. The important aspect was they were making a sincere gesture to their fellow mankind. It would only take a few minutes, and no one would ever know it was they who had placed the names there.

He was nearly finished when a deep voice called out from behind him. "Hey! What are you boys doing there?"

In this part of the country, horses were still one mode of power for farm work, and their near silent movement across the fields, allowed this farmer to approach unannounced. He didn't look too pleased with Steve's humanitarian act.

"I'm going to go ring up the cops. You can't be hacking up tombstones like that."

Before Steve could get out a response in an attempt to justify his actions, the farmer was well on his way toward a farm house, not too far away.

"Think he'll really call the cops?" Shawn asked.

"I *think* he looked real mad, and I *don't think* I'm going to stick around to find out if he's really got a telephone."

They picked up the pace considerably on the way back into town. Maybe the increase in industrialization did serve one good purpose. There were more places to get lost in the proverbial crowd. But as rapidly as rumors streaked through this town, the time to find a safe place to hide was probably minimal.

An open door on a boxcar near the end of the freight train just beginning to creep away from the down town depot was their invitation to a free ride part way back to Jasper Valley and the tunnel. Timing couldn't have been planned this perfectly. They didn't know if the '46 Ford police car cruising the area at a faster-than-casual rate was in pursuit of them, but at this point, there was no need to take any chances. As they tossed their duffel bags onto the deck of the rail car, two pairs of hands extended from around the corners of the open door, offering the much-needed assistance in climbing on board. It was one of the unwritten ethics of the nomadic drifters—the railroad bums—to help one another in a time of need, and these drifters had also seen the police car, and Shawn and Steve making their evasive maneuvers. It was apparently a time of need.

"Now get outa sight 'til we clear the city limits," one of them said, as Shawn and Steve scrambled to their feet and grabbed their bags, heeding the instructions from the more seasoned rail travelers.

There would only be time for brief introductions, as

the new-comers would disembark at the Lake Road crossing just a short distance out of town. They knew this train wouldn't have a full head of steam by that time, and just as inexperienced as they were at jumping off moving trains, they were quite sure they could do it.

The landings were a little awkward, but effective. The pre-jump lessons they received from the two rail riders whose names they couldn't recall five minutes later, let them hit the ground running. Their first train ride was quite brief, but grandly memorable.

TWENTY-THREE

I t would still be the middle of the night when they returned to their own time, so they wouldn't be faced with the problem of escaping the forbidden premises. Their flashlights, still stashed in the bottom of their duffels, should work again once they passed through the green light for the last time, to bring them back into 1965, but the candles were retained just in case. Their *Schwinns* were well-hidden and waiting, ready to transport them out to the lake, where they would sleep for the remainder of darkness, and then ride back into town for the usual Saturday morning malted milk at the drug store, as if nothing out of the ordinary had occurred.

All went as planned. Jasper Lake was the peaceful retreat it had always been to Shawn and Steve, and this place, this night, seemed more comforting and secure than it ever had, even before the incredible pilgrimage they had just endured, and survived. As they spread out Black Wolf's soft, supple blanket on the beach, their only hope was that they would not discover this had all been a wild dream when they awoke the next morning.

Westland was just as they had left it on the outset, and now it was time to pick up where they left off. The first stop *had* to be Otis Ramsey's soda fountain. They were long overdue treating their taste buds to one of his thick, creamy delights.

"Good morning, Otis," Shawn beamed with the anticipation of chunks of strawberries blended into Otis' cold, refreshing concoction.

"Mornin,' boys," Otis replied. "Where were you on Saturday? I missed you."

"But this is—"

Steve cut Shawn's statement short with a discrete poke in the ribs. Apparently, this *wasn't* Saturday, and until it was determined what day it really was, they'd better come up with some sort of deterrent to squelch the curiosity regarding their absence.

"We've been out camping, and I guess we must have lost track of the days," Steve said calmly. "I'll have chocolate, today."

"And I'll have strawberry, please," Shawn added.

Otis went to work at his usual, methodical pace, preparing the malteds, offering some friendly advice at the same time.

"You guys better let your folks know you're okay. They've been a little worried. They knew you were out camping, but they didn't know where. Yesterday, Mr. Kelly came in asking if I had seen you. He was ready to send out a posse looking for you."

Shawn chuckled. "I think there *was* a posse looking for us..."

Steve poked him in the ribs again.

Shawn quickly got the message. He dug into his pocket for some change to pay for his malt. Otis immediately recognized the two quarters as currency not of the present era, and he was even more curious when he saw Steve's remittance of similar vintage.

"Where did you get these? Are you sure you want to spend these old coins on ice cream?"

Steve was quick with a reply. "Um... we found them out in the woods where we were camping. It's all we got with us right now. Maybe you can hold them 'till we can bring in some other money."

Otis readily agreed to the terms. He wasn't going to pilfer from his two most loyal customers.

TWENTY-FOUR

Expecting a devastating reprimand now that it was Wednesday, Shawn meekly approached his father at the lumber yard, and in the most apologetic tone he could muster, he reused the excuse Steve had created at the soda fountain. "I guess we just lost track of the time."

Don Kelly was more relieved than he was angry. "Well, *next time*, at least let us know where you're going. We were worried. Now go let your mother know you're home."

Shawn and Steve were relieved, too. It hadn't been a dream. It was all as real to them as Westland was at that very moment. They now had all the ammunition to tell the actual saga, but who would ever believe it? Chances were pretty good that everyone would hear their story just as another version of an already established legend. Seventy-five years after the fact, there would be little concern by anyone for the two women who died at the hands of the Hawthornes. Nor, would there be any concern that the Hawthorne sisters had so cleverly eluded punishment for their crimes.

Late one afternoon, after nearly a week of making excuses to their friends for why they missed the softball game, and the big party out at the lake, Shawn and Steve sought the seclusion of the rocks on the west edge of town that still remained as one of their escapes from everyday frustrations. There, they could reflect on all they had learned without interruption, and recreate the entire account while it was still fresh in their minds.

Before they ascended to their favorite ledge, Steve circled around to the back side of the huge boulders, and quickly summoned Shawn to observe his discovery. There, nearly lost among the hundreds of etched and painted initials, names, dates, hearts and arrows that had accumulated over the years, was the weathered and worn "X" that Steve had chiseled into the stone, along with the four sets of initials, that recorded for all time the pact of secrecy they had made with Spencer Garett and Brady Pendleton.

If there was no other means to affirm the reality of their experience, to themselves, at least, this certainly indicated that Shawn and Steve had really been there *in 1890*. Steve dismissed the possibility of using it as proof. No one was going to believe this either.

They perched on their ledge, and recalled every incident in detail from the ride on the lumber wagon to their first meal at the Hotel; from the mysterious, fatal birthday party to the escape from Marshall Flagg's posse; from the brush with Capone to the visit to Dino's Cafe.

They reminded themselves of the remarkable friendships, brief as they were, to be everlasting, unforgettable impressions. They owed their lives to Spencer, Brady, and Jesse.

And who would ever believe a tale describing a scrape with Al Capone, or that the Indian blanket was actually obtained directly from the hands of Black Wolf?

They reminisced the phenomenal changes that occurred over the decades, and the incredible sights that, perhaps few people alive now, had ever witnessed. The church in its glorious frontier grandeur. The forest that nearly covered all of what is now the southern reaches of Westland. The log cabins and farms that eventually gave way to the High School, modern homes, a football field, and a baseball diamond.

A blacksmith shop, and a general store; the old, abandoned barn that protected them from a thunderstorm, and the steam locomotive; horses and buggies, and pickle barrels.

While sorting out the spectrum of details, Shawn and Steve realized they had not only seen historical Westland the way it really was. They had discovered, and solved a crime no one knew happened. They couldn't return to that era to report it. By now their likenesses were probably gracing the walls in Marshall Flagg's rogue gallery. As victims of circumstance, they were wanted criminals for the disappearance of Wilma Kerns and Alice Page in that time.

Not only had they solved the mystery of the three girls who vanished in 1929, they now knew why the Hawthorne house was never repainted, and why only the windows and doors on the back side of the house were boarded up.

With all the information they had gathered, Shawn and Steve were confident, now, that the Hawthorne ghost sightings in past years were the prostitutes. *"Had* to be them. They're the only ones who knew about the tunnel."

A thundering gang of ten-year-old cowboys being chased by a relentless tribe of screaming nine-year-old Indians were infiltrating the rocks. Perhaps it was time to relinquish daytime hours here to a new generation of cow pokes and savages. Somehow, even though they were losing their stronghold in this, their domain of solitude, Shawn and Steve graciously accepted the invasion. It was good to know the tradition lived on, and there was always the park gazebo, where the analysis could continue.

The solar rays were casting longer shadows now, but the old house had lost its element of luster, and its ability to capture a sunset in an array of radiant elegance, as Shawn and Steve had witnessed at this time of day, *once so long ago.* Now, it was nothing more than a drab, weather-beaten old wreck that was still living up to the legend. As Shawn and Steve sat there in the rose garden shelter, they took particular notice of several pedestrians across the street. Twenty feet before they reached the corner of the weed-filled lot, they abruptly changed course, crossed the street, and continued on past the park. When they were well beyond the parameters of their superstitious fear, they crossed back over the street, and resumed their original direction. Another Westland tradition lived on.

It was just about suppertime—time to enjoy a home-cooked meal in the company of family. Steve and his father were invited to join the Kellys that night for pork chops, mashed potatoes and gravy, and fresh corn-on-the-cob, right out of the Kellys' garden. That combination was one of Steve's favorites, and Kathy Kelly knew how to cook pork chops fit for a king.

Just as they were stepping off the gazebo, something caught Steve's eye.

"Shawn! I saw someone in the upstairs window. I'm not kidding!"

"What window?" Shawn asked, somewhat in disbelief. He thought Steve was just joking with him.

"The one where the pool table is."

"Could you tell who it was? Was it those girls?"

"I don't know, but who else could it be?" Steve was much too serious for this to be a prank. He had seen someone, *or something*, and Shawn accepted his sincerity.

At last, they had the opportunity to accomplish what they had set out to do so long ago, and they weren't going to sit through a thunderstorm to do it. Never before, in all of their attempts, had they ever caught as much as a glimpse of the slightest movement in any of those windows. Now they were not only going to see the ghosts. They were going to confront them. They knew who the visitors were, and there was absolutely nothing to fear.

They couldn't chance taking the long route to the railroad track. That might take too much time. They darted across the street and into the shadows of the back yard, around the corner of the house and to the cellar entrance, risking the chance of being seen in nearly broad daylight. But this was far too important to be concerned with that now.

They had been in and out of that cellar enough times to know exactly where they were going, even without a flashlight. They felt their way along the stone wall, right to the ladder steps. The trap door above was already open, and they were sure they had not left it that way. Not hesitating a second, they negotiated the steps up into the pantry. Through the kitchen and the library, into the parlor, and as if they were in their own house, they dodged past all the furniture and stood at the bottom of the stairway. This was it. The visitors had no other way out.

Suddenly, they heard the crack of the cue ball against the rack, and the clicking of several balls striking one another. Capone's table was getting use, after all these years of sitting idle. They cautiously ascended the darkened stairwell, desperately trying to gain sight of the players, but the filtered sunlight through the dirty windows did not reveal anything to them, until they nearly reached the top.

"You guys play Snooker? Been waiting for you. I was hoping you'd see me in the window and come on up."

Of all the adventures Shawn and Steve had experienced during the past couple of weeks, this had to be the most incredible discovery yet. They stood at the top of the stairs, so astonished they could hardly speak. This was not who they were expecting to see, and the one person farthest from their imagination to be the mystery guest. Could this possibly be the *ghost* who had mystified so many over the years? Was this the figure on whom the legend mongers had based their ghostly tales?

With cue stick in hand, and a Texas-sized smile, unquestionably happy to see Shawn and Steve, he ruffled his uncombed, short, blonde hair. "I didn't think I'd ever find you again... but I guess I finally did it. What year *is this*, anyway?"

"Nineteen sixty-five," Steve said, realizing now that Jesse was *really* there. Expecting two females they had never met, and with whom they would have little in common, instead, Jesse was a welcomed and pleasant surprise.

"How did you get here?" Shawn asked, overlooking the obvious. He was still in a state of total amazement.

"Same way you did. Through the tunnel."

"But how did you find out about it?"

"I've known about the tunnel for a long time, ever since Al was coming around, when Lizz and Emma were in his good graces. I discovered it once when I stashed a bunch of liquor in the cellar, but I never told the Hawthornes or anyone else that I knew about it. I thought Lizz and Emma and the girls they stole from Capone were the only ones who knew about it, until you two showed up in 1930."

"But how did you know we came through it?"

"I had seen you once before, on one of my trips to 1890. Thought you seemed a little misplaced. And then when you were sitting there in the park in '30, looking kind of lost, and just staring at the house, I knew right away how you had gotten there."

"So... what brings you to 1965?"

"I tried quite a few times, and I always wound up in the '50s, '57 mostly. That was pretty scary. I wandered around town a little then. Couldn't believe a newspaper cost thirty-five cents! I'd come back here and stay in the attic for a while, read the paper, and watch everything going on from the windows up there—nighttime mostly, so no one would see me. Sometimes the weather was so stormy I didn't want to go out anyway."

That explained the newspapers on the third floor. That explained the *ghosts* appearing during thunderstorms. And speculation created another conclusion: Shawn and Steve had widened the time spectrum by opening the portal into later years. They made it possible for Jesse to venture farther than 1957.

Steve looked at Shawn. "Then it wasn't the dam that caused the sightings to stop in '57."

"What sightings? What dam?" Jesse asked.

Steve explained the geographic change Jesse knew nothing about. "You know the valley at the other end of the tunnel? Well, in 1957 a flood control dam was built there. The tunnel entrance was covered, and that whole valley is a big lake now. At first we thought that was the reason no one had come through it since then."

Shawn continued with the explanation. "You see, up until '57, there were a few people who *did* see you in the windows during the storms. Everyone believed the ghosts of Emma and Lizzy Hawthorne were still in this house. There isn't a single person in this town who will even come near it... except us. And now they want to tear it down, and my dad wants to buy the land to expand his lumber yard."

"*Your Dad!* Don't the Kellys still own the lumber yard?"

"Don Kelly is my father."

Jesse displayed an expression of surprise, and Shawn realized he might have told more than he should have. But Jesse was a mature being, and he didn't express any hard feelings toward Shawn.

"I know your Dad very well. We practically grew up together, and I guess that makes your grandfather the man who took care of me when my Pop died. Mr. Kelly made sure I had everything I needed 'till I was old enough to start working. He even got me the job at the railroad depot." Steve sensed Shawn's uneasiness with the conversation. It was time to change the subject. "Did you know the Hawthornes killed those two ladies who were found in the house that day we were there?"

"I didn't know for sure, but I always suspected that's what happened."

"So what happened to Emma and Lizzy after we left?"

"They stayed at the Hotel for a week. Left every window in the house open to air it out. Then they left on the train again. That was almost a week ago."

"Did you ever get your Model A?"

"Sure did! Just a couple days ago. And now I'm getting ready to leave town, but I wanted to try one last time to find you."

Shawn shuddered to think Jesse would return to one of the grimmest periods of American history. "Why don't you stay here with us? Life is *much* better in 1965 than it was—*or is*—in 1930. And I'd bet my Dad would be really glad to see you again."

"Shawn, your father is fifty-some years old now, and I'm still just twenty. I don't think that would be a very good idea. Besides, your world looks way too complicated. I belong back there... where I'm supposed to be. I'll come back to visit your Dad when the time is right."

They were late for supper, but seeing Jesse again, and finding the last piece of the puzzle was well worth the mild scolding.

TWENTY-FIVE

Don Kelly was settled on the living room couch with every intention of catching up on the current events of the day, the newspaper spread out on his lap, and one ear tuned to the television ten o'clock news in front of him. Shawn didn't usually bother him during his nightly reading and listening routine, but tonight, the younger Kelly had some guilt feelings he had to unload, and lately, his father's busy season schedule left very little time to chat. They had always enjoyed and cherished a strong father/son bond, and even at the age of seventeen, Shawn still found it appropriate to sit shoulder-to-shoulder with his father on the couch, even if there was another four feet of empty couch available. And although he never mentioned it, Don wouldn't have wanted it any other way. He was proud of his offspring's academic accomplishments, but more than that, he was proud of the genuine person Shawn had become, and it was gratifying to know the family business would be passed on to capable and caring hands.

"Dad... I'm really sorry I've been a pain in the ass lately."

Don raised his eyebrows, but his eyes kept focused on the sports page. "What do you mean by that?"

"Well, last week when me and Steve went camping and we stayed out there longer than we should've... and tonight we got back late for supper... we didn't mean to do all that on purpose. It just happened."

"No harm done." Don turned the page to bury his real emotion in the financial section.

Shawn sensed the necessity for further explanation. "It's just that... well... this is our last summer before we graduate, and next year at this time I'll be going off to college somewhere and I suppose I'll be working most of the time next summer. This is our last chance to be just kids. You know what I mean?"

Mr. Kelly glanced away from the paper. He was impressed with Shawn's mature observation of accepting an implied responsible role in his not-so-distant adult future. That statement re-assured him that Shawn was headed for success, and as a little advance reward, he would recognize and respect Shawn's concern of wanting to be a *kid* for the rest of the summer.

"Yes, Shawn, I know exactly what you mean. I only wish I would've had that attitude when I was your age."

Shawn saw his opportunity to squeeze out a bit of information he had never heard his dad talk about.

"Me and Steve are probably just like you and Jesse were back then."

Don put down the paper, and a touch of astonishment took up residency on his face.

"Jesse! How do you know about Jesse?"

"Um... I guess I heard you mention him once or twice... and I just happened to think of it now."

Don rubbed his chin, and thoughts of his own youthful

years sparkled in his eyes.

"Jesse was a good friend. He lost his parents when he was very young. We took him in for a while, and your Grandpa Kelly treated him like one of his own. Those were hard times, but Jesse always managed to land on his feet... saved all his money, and one day he pulled up in front of the lumber yard in a brand new Model A Ford... *had* to show it to Grandpa Kelly before anyone else.   He was so proud of that car. Not too long after that, he left town, and I don't know where he ever ended up. Never saw him after that."

Now Shawn knew he shouldn't expect to see Jesse playing Snooker in the Hawthorne house again. Today must've been *his* last trip through the tunnel. But another thought occurred to Shawn, one that might brighten his father's spirit.

"You never know!   Maybe he'll show up again someday... and he'll probably be driving a Lincoln."

TWENTY-SIX

With less than a month until school began for another year, there hardly seemed time for all the usual summertime activities, much less, a visit to a nursing home. But Steve insisted that Shawn come with him. He had been there with his father the day before visiting a distant relative he hardly knew, and noticed something there that Shawn had to see for himself.

Westland Nursing Home was one of the most recent, modern additions to the city's outskirts. From outward appearances it looked more like an apartment building, but inside the main entrance, there was no mistaking this facility for nothing short of a hospital.

Shawn was completely in the dark. He had no idea why Steve had drug him into this place overflowing with people he did not recognize, and Steve wasn't giving him the slightest clue. But he trusted Steve's judgment, and when they reached the nurses' station at the east wing, and Steve asked the attendant there "Is it okay if we visit the gentleman in room one twenty-four?" Shawn was confident Steve knew what he was doing.

"Sure. I'll bet he'd love to have some company today," the nurse said with a smile, and pointed them down the corridor.

"Thank you, Ma'am. I know where it is."

They approached the open door, and Steve pointed to the name plaque on the wall next to it. Suddenly, the fog lifted from this secretive mission, as Shawn read the name.

His hair was white, and his face held a pale, withdrawn expression. His body was frail and weak, and the movements were slow and deliberate, as he made his way from the window to the plush, high-backed arm chair, carefully lowering himself into it. *Brady Pendleton* was 89, and he had returned to Westland to live out his final years.

The burden of explaining who they were, and why they were there, would be the most difficult task Shawn and Steve had faced. Without any preparation, they weren't even sure where to begin.

"Hello, Mr. Pendleton."

"Hello, Brady."

The old man remained comfortably seated in his chair with a custom hand-carved, highly polished wooden cane resting against the chair front between his knees.

"Hello, boys," he replied, seemingly delighted to have visitors.

Before Steve could begin speaking again, Mr. Pendleton was reaching for a pair of eye glasses on the small nightstand beside him. He put on the spectacles, and obviously studying the two lads standing before him he asked, "Don't I know you two from somewhere?"

"Yes, Brady... you do. I'm Steve."

"And I'm Shawn."

Steve began to realize this might not be so difficult, after all.

"You and Spencer... a campfire in the woods across the

road from the Hawthorne house. You'd been fishing at Miller's Pond. The next day we split firewood out behind the Blacksmith Shop, and then we all went swimming at Raccoon Holler. And then we all came back and ate supper at Spencer's house."

Brady Pendleton just sat calmly, listening intently to every word.

Shawn continued with the seventy-five-year-old itinerary. "The next day, we saw Black Wolf on the street, and I bought the blanket from him. And that night we saw the Hawthorne twins poison those two other women and haul the bodies away in a buggy behind a white horse..."

Steve intervened. "Cleo. The horse's name was Cleo. He came from P.T. Barnum's Circus."

Brady's face was beaming with joyous amazement as Shawn went on.

"Then we all took an oath of secrecy, and Steve and I had to hide in Garett's hay loft and you and Spencer rode us out to the valley and led the posse that was chasing us up the valley so we could get away."

Brady didn't know how these two boys, in 1965, could possibly have all this information. They certainly appeared as the two drifters he remembered, and the events they were describing were quite vivid memories he had carried with him throughout his lifetime. But there was *one* detail they couldn't possibly know. It would be the final test of their validity.

"But before you left that night..." Brady paused, to

carefully choose the right words. "You gave me something. Do you remember?"

Shawn smiled. He knew he was being tested. "I gave you a five-dollar gold piece, for good luck."

"And I gave one to Spencer, too," Steve added.

Brady pulled open a drawer in the nightstand, and when his hand emerged, it was holding the two Half Eagles, brightly polished, and each strung on gold neck chains. He held them out for Shawn and Steve to examine.

"I don't know how it's possible. *No one* could have known that. We never told *anyone.*"

"Why do you have both pieces?" Steve asked. "Where is Spencer?"

The old man's face turned a little sad. "Spencer gave me his just before he died about three years ago. "We always figured they *really were lucky.* As long as we had these things hanging around our necks, good things happened. Then one day, Spencer left his in his room... out in Portland we were, working on the riverboats on the Columbia. The dang fool slipped and fell on a loading dock and broke his dad burn leg."

"So what have you been doing all these years?" Shawn asked.

"Just after World War One, we bought our own boat. *Northern Lights* we called her. Ferried cars and passengers across the bay at Astoria every day for thirty-three years. Never will forget the day we made our last trip and retired... November third, 1951."

The entire afternoon just slipped away as Shawn and Steve, like children hearing bedtime stories, listened to Brady's tales of the true wild, wild West. His ability to deliver them was just as entertaining now, as it had been the first night they met. Only now, his English had improved.

As they were preparing to leave, with the promise to visit again soon, Brady requested his long lost friends to come close to his side, and as they honored his petition, he draped the golden chains around their necks. "Hang on to these... *for good luck*... I want *you* to have them now, and I know Spencer would, too."

Only Shawn and Steve would ever really know the true meaning of these tokens. Although the actual value was great, to them, the gold coins were priceless in terms only they could understand.

Steve pulled out his pocket watch just as a nurse came into the room to check on Mr. Pendleton.

"Wow! Where did you get that neat watch?" she asked as she admired the handsome timepiece.

Steve just smiled. "The Emporium... at the other end of the tunnel."

ABOUT THE AUTHOR

Born into a farm family in the late 1940s, J.L. Fredrick lived his youth in rural Western Wisconsin, a modest but comfortable life not far from the Mississippi River. His father was a farmer, and his mother, an elementary school teacher. He attended a one-room country school for his first seven years of education.

Wisconsin has been home all his life, with exception of a few years in Minnesota and Florida. After college in La Crosse, Wisconsin and a stint with Uncle Sam during the Viet Nam era, the next few years were unsettled as he explored and experimented with life's options. He entered into the transportation industry in 1975 where he remained until retirement in 2012

Since 2001 he has thirteen published novels to his credit, and one non-fiction history volume, *Rivers, Roads, & Rails.* He was a featured author during Grand Excursion 2004.

J.L. Fredrick currently resides at Poynette, Wisconsin.